TROLLING THE

WOE

ILLUSTRATED COMMENTARY, COMEDY & COUPLETS FROM RADIOFREEOZ.COM

BY
PETER BERGMAN
WITH
DAVID OSSMAN

ILLUSTRATED BY
PHIL FOUNTAIN

Dedicated to Mr. Voot, who remains
forever in my heart

PREFACE

Trolling The Woe is a collection of the best of the writings and cartoons featured on Radio Free Oz from its Web inception on April 22, 2010 thru June of 2011. RadioFreeOz.com posted its first show on Earth Day, just days before the BP oil spill. Oz is still with us; but you will search in vain for articles on the BP disaster in the mainstream press, as if it no longer remained a massive threat when it was overtaken in the news cycle by the drivel of the boobs running for Congress, or the antics of the glitterati, pushing each other aside for their moment in the media sun. The Gulf is dying along with other vast stretches of the world's oceans (our largest farm), but if the poisoned tide isn't tossing up oil drenched water fowl or rolling tar balls on our beaches, America's greatest, man made, natural disaster isn't apparently worth the ink or the bandwidth to cover it. But, fear not, The Great Oz never forgets.

Radio Free Oz first went on the air in 1966 on KPFK, Los Angeles' listener sponsored Pacifica station, just as the "hippie revolution" was rising from the smoke. The Firesign Theatre was born on Oz in the fall of that year, and on Easter Sunday 1967, in Elysian Park, Oz staged the first Love In. Fifty thousand people showed up-I expected five. For the last forty-five years, Radio Free Oz has been on and off the air, fired twice by the same radio station, once for being too radical, once for not being not radical enough.

Oz has always been a team effort, and its digital incarnation is no exception. David Ossman, my Firesign brother, co-hosts the weekly long-form show, Phil Fountain turns politics into pixels, Tom Gedwillo masters our Website, Tom O'Neill designs it, Scott Wild keeps us thoroughly socially networked and Chas Glass deftly handles the books.

Enjoy this compilation, stay tuned to Radio Free Oz and, in these "interesting times" remember our motto, "We're Going To Get Through This Together."

Peter Bergman
Los Angeles 2011

TABLE OF CONTENTS KEY

GSK	GUARANTEED SUBATANCE FREE
GTO	GET THIS ONE PARTY STARTED
HTB	A HOOT TO BOOT
HTR	LET'S PLAY "HIDE THE TERRORIST"
ING	INTO THE GREAT BLUE WONDER
MHA	MAD HATTERS AT THE T-PAWTY
MM	MISSING MIKEY
MMN	MY MIDTERM NIGHTMARE
MOM	MIDTERM OF OUR MADNESS
MYN	MY WAY AND NO HIGHWAYS
NCW	THE GRAY AND THE BROWN-THE NEW CIVIL WAR
NND	THE NEW NEW DEAl: TAX POLICY
NTA	NONE OF THE ABOVE
NTP	NO TOM PAINE, NO GAIN
NWC	NO, WE CANTOR
NUF	NEWT'S UNFRIENDLY FIRE
OAP	OBAMA-AFGHANISTAN-PAKISTAN: THE GREAT CONFORMANCE
ODM	OSAMA'S DEAD-MEDUSA'S NEXT
ONS	ON NOVEMBER 2ND, DO THE RIGHT THING
OPM	THE VIEW FROM OIL PEAK MOUNTAIN
PBF	PLAN "B" FOR THE GOP
PTG	PICKING THE GRIDLOCK
PTP	A STROLL DOWN THE PATH TO PROSPERITY
PTO	PUNKING THE GOP
RCB	EMPIRE JEOPARDY RED CLOAK FOR BREAKFAST
RSE	ROCK SNOT ELLEGY

TABLE OF CONTENTS

Koch Brothers OAP, NTP, GTO, MYN, DMP, PBF

Phyllis Schlafly ANF

Don Imus TCM

Joe Miller HTB, CTB

Meg Whitman MMN

Carly Fiorina MMN

Carl Paladino MMN

Darrell Issa PTG

Rupert Murdoch FNF

Tom Tancredo CTB

Donald Trump TSB, SUG, TNM

Larry Summers DMP

Tim Coburn DOW

BAD GUYS

Al Qaeda WOT, BDM, NCW, ODM, HTR

Corporate America TBH, RTM, TPG, GTA, PTG

Dubya ONS, GFA, GTO, DTO, DAD, AYD

Fox News FNF

Osama Bin Laden BBT, ODM, DAD, TLR

Taliban OAP, WOT, BBT, RTM

Terrorists, Insurgents, Militants TME

Kadafi SID

DISASTERS-PAST, PRESENT AND FUTURE

Abu Ghraid FAH, RSE, TLR

Cataclysmic Purification of America RCB, OPM

Gulf Oil Spill SLS, RCB, NTA, ABE, MMN

DISLOYAL OPPOSITION

Mitch McConnell DTJ, NTA, TNM, PTO, FFF, DTO

John Boehner (The Tan Woodman) GFA, CTB, PTG, TSB, PTP, TNM, FFF, TCC, NFA, BDM, OPM, PTO

Eric Cantor PTG, NWC, PTO

GOOD GUYS

Joe Biden DTI, ATU

Jerry Brown MMN

Richard Byrd DTI

Barbara Boxer MMN

Andrew Cuomo MMN

Russ Feingold HTB, MMN

Nancy Pelosi GTO

Harry Reid MMN, PTP, TMP,

OBAMA (THE NOT ME)

MOM, DBM, OAP, TCC, NTP, MMN, GFA, PTG, ATU, NTA, GTO, TSB, PTO, AOW, NWC, SID, DTO, TNM, ING, DMP, MM, PBF, ONS, NCW, CTB, GSK

PIPE DREAMS

Abstinance DTA, OAP

American Exceptionalism NCW, AOW

The Big Tent GTO, ABE, ING

RABBLE ROUSERS

Rush Limbaugh NCW, GTO, TNM

Glenn Beck   NCW TCM, FNF, NTA, GTP

Laura Schlesinger   NCW

Bill O'Reilly MMN, FNF

Sean Hannity MMN, FNF

SPAWN OF SATAN

Death Panels DII, PTP

Gay Marriage NTA

Homosexuals ANF

Masturbation DTA, OAP, AWF,

Obamacare OAP, WOT, DII, NCW, FNF, NTA

The Stimulus WOT, ONS

TARP WPT, ONS

Witches ANF

THE ECONOMY

Double Dip ONS, NTT, NCW, DLS, NND, GTO

The Fed STC

Lord MaynardKedynes TSU

Paul Ryan & "The Path To Prosperity" MYN, PTO, PTP, TMP, NUF, TSU, PBF

THE GARDEN GNOMES

Sarah Palin, ANF, DII, FNF, NTA, SUG, DHC

Ron Paul MMN, EDH, DOW, PBF,

Mitt Romney NTA, SUG, MHA, PBF, GSK

Tim Pawlenty NTA, SUG, MHA. PBF

Michelle Bachmann TSB, DHC, SID, PBF, GSK

John Huntsman MHA

Herman Cain DHC, PBF

Rick Perry SDS

Rick Santorum PBF

WAR ZONES

Afghanistan AG, WOT, HTR, SID, BBT, RTM, DLS, OAP

Pakistan BBT, SID, TLR, HTR, OAP

Iraq OAP, TLR

Libya SID

WHACKOS

The Tea Party DBM, OAP, TCC, ONS, NTP, NCW, HTB, MMN, CTB, NND, NTA, ABE, ING, DHC, MHA, GTO, NTA, MYN

Pastor Terry Jones FAH

Christine O'Donnell DTA, ANF, HTB, CTB, MMN

Sharon Angle DTA, MMN, CTB, HTD

Ron Johnson HTB, MMN

Carl Paladino HTB

Jan Brewer MMN

Freshmen Republicans

Freshmen Republicans MYN

Newt Gingrich FAH, PBF, SUG, CTB, NUF, MYN, NTA, DTJ, DOW

John Bolton SID

Hal O'Dalí

THE MIDTERM OF OUR MADNESS

Bergman's Blog, September 4, 2010

So, all the pundits and the polls tell us that we are going to see a whole lot fewer Democrats in the congress after the midterm elections.

If the Dems are reduced to slim margins in both houses, then there will have to a whole new game plan laid down by Pelosi & Reid. It's all going to have to be done by reconciliation-51% does it.

We will be facing a '30s style depression, wearing a different style of glad rags. You don't have to be camera center in a Walker Evans photograph to be a player in the New Depression. And while we're waiting for the stimulus economy to kick in, we're going to have to find a way to support the families and individuals who are caught in the changeover.

The Republicans haven't a clue, because they have given up the hard work of planning for and working towards the betterment of the Commonwealth.

It will get real bad, real soon after the midterms, and suddenly everyone will be looking for some way to get through the transition from a totally unsustainable life style to something that works.

No easy transition; but sitting around blaming the "not me" is not going to do it. Being clever about how to get by with less, grow or make your own, bring people together, get off the grid-whatever-is going to get really sexy. Can't say, "I can hardly wait," because I'm hardly going to have to wait for this to happen.

DON'T BLAME ME, BLAME THE NOT- ME

Bergman's Blog, September 6, 2010

As I scan the media preparing for a new show-I call it "trolling the woe"-I am increasingly convinced that five months ago I gave the American people far too much credit for common sense, and thoroughly overrated their ability to recognize their own best self interests and see the bigger picture at the same time.

I figured all those pudgy, white, middle class boobs dressed up as George Washington lite would self-destruct and return to the flat screen reality they left at home.

I failed to factor in The Entitlement Quotient. I didn't calculate the distance from high up on the hog where a whole lot of Americans have been living to the common ground below. What a leap of faith! You could bust up your unconscious, unsustainable lifestyle taking a jump like that.

So they whine and wimper, why is everything suddenly falling apart? What happened to all our endless home equity. platinum credit and bulging 401 k's? It can't be our fault, we're the heroic 5% of the world's population consuming 25% of the world's resources.

It's a conspiracy-we're victims of the Not-Me. That Not-Me Obama, who's going to build a mosque on the top of the White House and call us all to Health Care. That Not-Me the immigrant, who's out stealing the jobs we won't take. That Not-Me the progressive, who's really Che in Mao's clothing, or Hitler cross dressing as Stalin.

All we have to do is vote everybody out of office, and then wait until somebody gives us back our constitution and our good old way of life.

How dare these half baked couch potatoes usurp the noble brand of the Boston Tea Party! They're not putting their livlihood and personal safety at risk with a brave act of civil disobeience in the face of hostile, occupying troops. They're not up on Bunker Hill trading bullets with the British army. They're nothing more and nothing less than a gaggle of angry drones being joysticked by bigots and billionaires.

EAT THE RICH:
BURN THE BUSH TAX CUTS
Bergman's Blog, September 9, 2010

I was performing with Phil Proctor in Madison, Wisconsin in the mid 70's sharing the bill with Patti Smith. Driving into the venue's parking garage I was treated to a large graffiti that read EAT THE RICH. I thought it was apt then, and I think it's a whole lot more apt now.

The economic cancer that's eating away at our society is the unbelievable and ultimately unbearable income disparity between the rich and everyone else.

In 1915 when we were displacing Britain as the richest nation on the planet, our wealthiest 1% accounted for 18% of the nation's income. Today, that figure is an outrageous 24%. The widening of this chasm wasn't spread out over the century; it erupted in the last two decades.

And now, here we are, going broke state by state, business by business, household by household, individual by individual while a small, tight knit cabal of multi-millionaires and multi-multi millionaire take control of the political process.

The most politically conservative Supreme Court since the New Deal decided that money, regardless of how much is gathered at one point to do the damage is "free speech," unleashing the ultra-rich Super PAC's, with the jovial, ever-jowly Karl Rove running with the big dogs again.

Thank DARPA or Dharma (your choice) for the Internet, an Excaliber pulled out of the lake just in time to do battle with this tax-free propaganda juggernaut and Fox's stable of hydra-deaded hooligans and alter boy bullies.

At some level of their consciousness, the super rich, along with everyone else knows that the whole thing is coming apart. The response since the Bush Coup Lite in 2004 has been a pell mell rush to fascism. Not the black leather and strut fascism of Benito Mussolini. America is developing its own brand, with it's own icons and its own enemies.

But it's fascism nonetheless--the conflation of government, finance , military and the conclave of Christian Ayatollahs appearing in mega churches and mall fronts everywhere.

Right now, Brand New American Fascism is doing just fine, because the bulk of the people who can and will eventually do something about it are still in shock. No surprise. It all happened pretty fast, and at the end of an equity bubble that was a soft ride for anybody with any real estate on them at the time. Boom Dot Burst! All gone. No beuno.

Now, we have to pull ourselves together, and solve this on our own. We can't wait for big government, Wall Street, the DOD/CIA and the Inerrant to play house with us. Their tools and toys are so big and expensive that they choose to play only with each other, but with our money.

There's nothing immoral, unethical or unnatural about a 95% tax rate for super wealth, a lifting of the corporate veil (aren't we in AfPak to life veils?), a moratorium on all domestic drilling and a decommissioning of all nuclear weapons.

We're not alone. There is a ready contingent of hackers, home boys, Hecates and heroes waiting in the wings to help get the New New Deal off the ground.

FEAR AND HATE 451 - NO MATCH TO MOHAMMED

Bergman's Blog, September 12, 2010

So, Pastor Terry Jones has upped his "Q" another mega-level by going on the *Today Show* and telling the world he isn't going to throw his 9/11 Koran Burning Party after all.

A patriotic pie in the face to the show's producers for giving in to this toxic wing-nut's blackmail. All Terry had to do was threaten a mean, senseless, wildly damaging act that barely qualifies within the Bill Of Rights and bingo, he's on the front page on the daily fish wrap, pumped full of Google Juice, Huff And Puffed, blogged within an inch of his life, and on the couch between Lady Gaga and Sharon Osbourne telling David, Jay and Conan why he decided not to put a match to Mohammed.

What puts the extra "Oh!" in this odious scenario is that the Rev did not heed the advice of his President, the General in charge of the AfPak crusade, every other Christian in Gainesville and Mama Bear herself until the very last moment.

Never mind the mobs in Kabul calling for my death (I am an American); never mind the brigade of youth turned to jihad because of this egregious provocation; Pastor pyromaniac has quickened the late summer news cycle and made a thousand column inches bloom.

Permitting him to preen and posture on camera as he prepares to put the torch to someone else's truth is a demonstration loud and clear of the resilience and capacity of our democracy, the very product we're importing abroad to the millions of "someone elses."

And, in a better world-one in which we gathered up our failed policies and spent uranium and returned home to take care of our own-the story of how we let Terry be Terry in the name of free speech and personal freedom would be told in every girls' school we had built from the Kandahar to Karachi.

But, no, this flexing of our muscular system of civil liberties was obscured by the chorus of anti Muslim rhetoric emanating from the nasty crowds at Ground Zero, the troubled mind of Newt Gingrich and the poisonous preachings of Franklin Graham. (Oh, that Billy had not given us his only son.)

What's next? Surely Reverend Terry's public relations triumph has produced a litter of copy cats. They're going to have to belly up and lift the bar of desecration if they expect to get any respect from the jaded pharaohs of journalism.

The resources are there; just browse the slideshow from Abu Ghraib. All it takes is a little imagination and a willing press. See you on the other side.

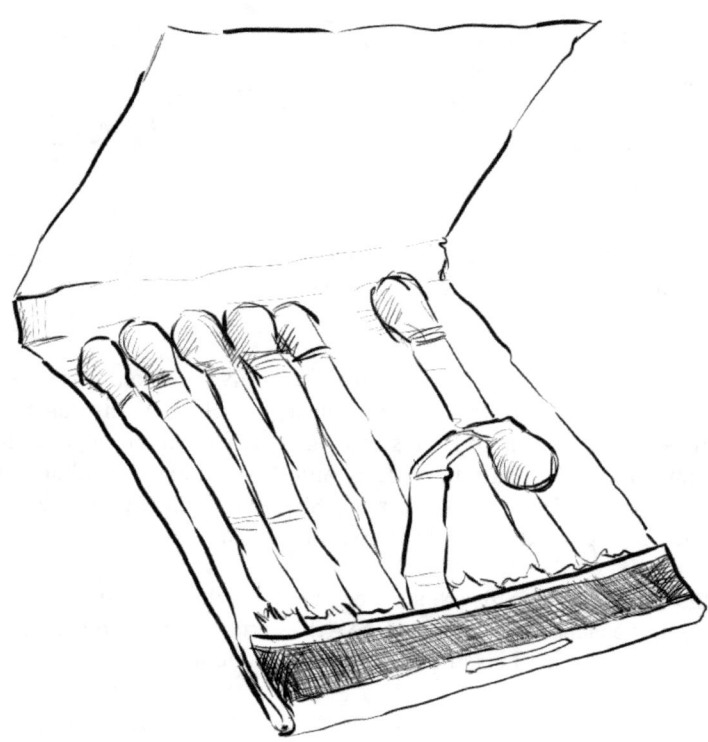

Written & Performed by Peter Bergman and David Ossman
Audio Production by Dave Malony

HOST: We're backstage talking to the winner of "Afghan Gladiator," the hot new TV show that gives returning vets from AfPak a chance to go back for another tour of counter-insurgency. Here he is, a former National Guardsman who has already revolved through eight tours over there – PTSD 1st   Class, Crystal McStanley. Tell us about yourself, Chris . . .

CHRIS: Yes, sir. Well, I joined up at 18 for on-the-job training, and it sure was, because three days later I was in Kandahar. I want to go back, but they said I'm too used up, so I guess this shows 'em.

HOST: I suppose you brought home some souvenirs from your last tour, right?

CHRIS: Sure – aphasia, night sweats, the crabs, and I used to be a woman, but the Army took care of that, last time I looked.

HOST: Chris, tell me about the "Afghan Gladiator" challenge.

CHRIS: First there was the pop-up fire-fights – I got 5 points for every turban, lost 5 for every CD – that's collateral damage. I ended up even.

Then there was the IED swamp – I had to drain the thing and replace it with a girl's school.

Then came Bribe the Warlord – you, know – it's tea-up or get terminated on the Kabul to Freakin' Nowhere Hiway. Cost me an arm and a leg. Glad they weren't mine.

HOST: So you survived the first three challenges, how did it end up?

CHRIS: In the Poppy Field. You have to dream your way out of it.

HOST: Kinda like the war. How d'ja do it?

CHRIS: I used my big jar-head of Fratris-Ade –it's got meth-enhanced electrolytes to keep me up all night. See, you gotta stay up all day because the other guys own the night.

HOST: So what did you win, besides your chance to go back to Afghanistan?

CHRIS: A case of Bud Light Lime – enough to get the General from Paris to Berlin in my new Hummer.

HOST: The Army gave you a Hummer?

CHRIS: No, just the down payment. But it's got robusted air-conditioning and skin seats.

HOST: So that's your job on tour #9? Just driving the General?

CHRIS: No, sir. I'm a Stryker. Our orders are to Clear, Hold and Forget About It.

HOST: But what about winning the war?

CHRIS: There's no winning, sir. Just survival.

HOST: And, PTSD 1st Class, Chrystal McStanley, that's just what you've done on Afghan Gladiator today. Good luck on you way back to 'Stan. By the way, all those countries out there are called "Stan" something. What does that mean, did they tell ya?

CHRIS: Yes sir. "Stan" is Moslem for "pain." Afghani-pain, Uzbeki-pain, Paki-pain.

HOST: Well, no pain, no gain.

CHRIS: Lots of one, none of the other. But it's a good war, sir. I've already signed up my unborn children to forget about what I'm goin' out to clear and hold.

HOST: And back to you from the Bob Hopeless Studios in Burbank.

SLICK SHRIMP

Bergman's Blog, September 13, 2010

Author's Note: David and I wrote and produced Slick Shrimp for Oz when the BP oil was still gushing, and people were still paying attention.

PETER: I'm here on the shore of the Gulf Coast for Radio Free Oz, talking with Charles Dunder, the latest member of Obama's Gang Of Five sent down here to solve the oil spill crisis. You've just arrived here, haven't you Charles.

DANDER: Yes, I replaced Professor Katz the astrophysicist when it was revealed that he was a virulent homophobe and a climate change denier.

PETER: So, what do you add to the team?

DANDER: I run the Petro Nutritional Institute back at Solid State University. I'm down here investigating a sustainable solution to the massive loss of fish and shellfish that's going on as we speak.

PETER: Petro Nutrition? I'm not familiar with the field.

DANDER: It's relatively new-it didn't take off until we got the whole pertophilic nano-cloning process down.

PETER: Excuse me.

DANDER: Simply put, given the right starter genes, chain-ganged polymers and robust steroids, we can create a host of creatures that not only survive in oil-saturated water, but thrive on it.

PETER: Is that one of then—that thing you're holding in your hand-it looks vaguely like a shrimp.

DANDER: We call it the Slick Shrimp. And yes, it thrives in oil polluted wetlands. You throw a million Slick Shrimp scat--that's what they're called when they come out of the test tube no bigger than a poppy seed—and a month later, they're as big as Buster here and ready to be flavored and sent to market. Want to try one?

PETER: It's a little chewey…

DANDER: That's the polymer filling. How does it taste?

PETER: Tastes like pork.

DANDER: Yep, pork flavored slick shrimp-one of my favorites. Let me have it back.

PETER: Okay.

DANDER; See, I just dip it in the degreaser, and watch it spring back to life. Rub a little of this on it, and, now give it a try.

PETER: Hmmmm, now *that* tastes like jumbo bayou scampi-the real thing.

DANDER: They're all the real thing. Should go over real good with the green crowd-you can re-eat them up to a dozen times before the steroid skeleton breaks down and they turn to mush.

PETER: It's a reasonable short-term solution; but I can't wait for the real shrimp to return.

DANDER: Return?! Pete, that hole on the ocean floor is spewing 200,000 gallons of oil a day. Your great grandchildren will be waiting for the shrimp to return. Now, let's get real. Here's one of the Oil Happy Catfish I'm developing. Just put a match to it and poof! it's sautéed and ready to serve.

PETER: This is Peter Bergman at the Gulf for Radio Free Oz and I wanna go home.

ROCK SNOT ELEGY

Ossman's Blog, September 14, 2010

Hello, Dear Friends! This won't always be a poetry blog, but I thought you'd like to read the latest "news poem" I read on Oz recently. The double-spacing makes it a little long, but you can manage that. Oh, and "rock snot" is an invasive algae. -D.O.

ROCK SNOT ELEGY

1.

rock snot travels on felt-soled boots

the long-haired man with green eyes

blew his body right in two

got it on my phone

50 dead men all around and

their blood everywhere

mingled with loose change

broken watches

bits of the "cowardly attacker"

(whichever half)

his head stuck on a fruitstand down the block

2.

rock snot keeps moving stream to stream

Southward softly

on felt-soled shoes

the over-dressed windbag with stupid hair

gets a hung jury

so goes Old Chi Town

and down South in Juarez a smear

of red, white and blue blood

thickens on the pavement

policia

loitering

and a woman keens over the body whom

we'll never know

as the Drug War goes on smokin'

across some desert border grid where nothin' grows

3.

rock snot

one diatomic cell at a time

takes over

Cape Cod

one day watermelons next day slime

this guy Ramzi bin al-Shibh

doesn't look like a guy you'd trust to mow your lawn

Bugs Bunny teeth

khol-eyed, droopy lidded, stoned perhaps on

God Himself

a bad bad guy closeted in Cuba since ought-six

who

by now must know which way to face

by the arrows CIA painted on the prison floors

and surely has finished his

lessons

on how

to

apply for a job opportunity in   Yemen?

here's the thing

the CIA had that piece of rock snot in a prison

they built

in Morocco

kif capital of the World!

How did that happen? If I paid taxes I'd wonder . . .

a bad bad Tom Cruiser of a purple plot

a make believe Sly's still here muscle

man gun car prison human hero movie

all about this guy Ramzi from Old Shibh Town

who

didn't have a chance to go down

to the local unemployment line

and part himself piously body from soul

because like Bing and Bob the CIA could ship him off

Morocco bound

4.

That's how the rock snot moves

one long-haired green-eyed bomber at a time

one hung jury

one more body in the street

one bad bad guy

one CIA prison in Morocco at a time

one felt sole

at a time

and when you need "a break from America"

when it gets really scary around your money or your life

there's always Abu Dhabi

and the Blackwater Princes

that's where the rock snot dies

on the soles of

tough

leather

boots

David Ossman - from NYT 8/18-19/10

DON'T TELL ABE ABOUT CHRISTINE O'DONNELL

Bergman's Blog, September 15, 2010

 f course I know how small a state Delaware is; but never figured on how many small minds reside there.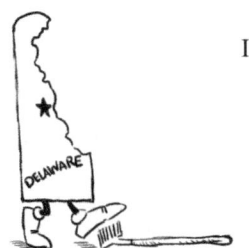

They've nominated a candidate to run for the Senate on the GOP ticket (don't tell Abe Lincoln, his casket RPM's are red-lining already) who under any other circumstances would be labeled Demented-Lite and laughed off the stage.

But this is the fall, and soon winter, of our discontent and Christine O'Donnell makes a whole lot of sense to people who have very little of their own.

Okay, she denies evolution and claims the Big Guy made the world in six 24/7's. No surprise. Her party tried to put a woman in the White House, one myocardial heartbeat away from The Button, who claims to have seen fossils commingled with the feet of giant dinosaurs and little children, proving they frolicked together in the the Scripture's not too distant past.

Okay, she thinks abstinence is a workable solution, despite all the statistics and single mothers to the contrary. No biggie. Christine knows statistics are the foot soldiers of secular science, who serve only the elite and their minions of smarter-than-thou intellectuals.

Okay, she claims masturbation is sexual perversion, despite millions of happy testamonials from those of us who beat off to a different drum.

None of her whacko ways disqualify her from running for office. What they would do in a better and saner time would disqualify her in the minds of any voter who took the time to figure out that putting an ignorant, bible-beating, retro cheerleader in the Senate is reckless and stupid.

Imagine making her one of the one hundred votes that peoples the Supreme Court, funds the War On The Not-Me, giveth or taketh away the bread from the needy and stands guard with our Founding Fathers at the sacred border between church and state.

Should she ascend to the senior chamber, she might find birdbrains of a feather if Rand Paul (rumored to be the love child of Ron Paul and Ayn Rand) and Sharron Angle surf home on this wave of fear and anger.

Christine can join Jim Inhofe and hotly deny global warming; help what's left of John Mc-Cain finish That Dang Fence and complement a feast of choice tax cuts for the rich with an after dinner Jim DeMint.

Remember, little minds can achieve great things if great minds do little to stop them.

OBAMA AFGHANISTAN PAKISTAN:
THE GREAT CONFORMANCE
Bergman's Blog, September 16, 2010

 oom! Boom! Lots of media thunderbolts shooting from the GOP's late summer, grassroots thunderstorm.

Yeah, "grassroots." The only thing grassroots about the Koch brothers, who are joy sticking half the dufusses's making the noise, is the mega-lawns they own and do not mow, and the toxic roots of the multi-billions they are loath to share.

Clap after clap , headline after headline tagging the sky: TAXES-HEALTH CARE-AB-STINENCE-MASTURBATION-KENYAN ANTI-COLONIALISM. This wall of anger is remarkable for the tags that are missing: AFGHANISTAN-PAKISTAN-TALIBAN-IRAQ-COLLECTING FINGERS-DRONING INSURGENTS-UNWINABLE UNAF-FORDABLE WAR.

How come the nobodies in the George Washington costumes and the camo-wife beater ensembles aren't complaining about the Dogs Of War? They're still unleashed, taking wikileaks on our official explanation for everything.

Why aren't they hounding Commander In Chief Obama? It's where he's most vulnerable. As a war leader Barack's a miserable failure. He can run the Harvard Law Review, organize Chicago's South Side, socialize medicine, buy General Motors and sell it back; but he doesn't have a scintilla of West Point or Lang-ley in him. He's an outsider who's inherited a concocted "global war on terror" run by a militarizing CIA and an increasingly covert DOD.

The Tea Party in not giving B. Hussein a pass out of kindness. They hate him the way the right hated FDR. As a child, a friend's mother gave me directions not to the toilet, but "The Roosevelt." Fast forward to a parade in Central Washington last week, where a bunch of yobs ran a float with a fellow yob in an Obama mask whipping the white guy who was pulling the cart-a chilling shade of medieval mummery that traditionally ends in Hellmouth.

They hate him, all right; but they treat him as if he and his shabbos goy, Petraeus are dispensational, and gladly grant them all the time and money in the world to finish what can't be finished and win what can't be won.

The Baggers are not alone, they are but a a subset of The Great Conformance.

Of the 535 members of Congress, only a handful have put the lie to the quagmire in Af-ghanistan and Pakistan and challenged the endless transfusion of blood and treasure that keeps the monster alive.

There is no anti-war movement roiling the streets because it's all so covert and the victims are from the other side of the world or the other side of town.

I say: End The AfPak Occupation Now, and kill the Deficit Hawks and the Endless War Hawks with one stone-one true stone to take down the Frankenstein that is stalking our future.

WHICH ONE IN THE TURBAN IS GEORGE WASHINGTON?
Bergman's Blog, September 19, 2010

 n my last blog I pondered why the vast majority in this country are so apparently unconcerned about the crusade we've been waging in Afghanistan for the past twenty-five years.

It's a first class disaster, yet people don't hate it the way they hate TARP, Obama-Care and The Stimulus; even though TARP saved us-at least for the time being-from a 30's style depression, Obama-Care ended the nightmare of no health coverage for 32 million Americans and The Stimulus put 800 billion dollars where our mouth belongs-in the greening and regeneration of a nation going rapidly to rust and ruin.

And then Oz Producer Bill McIntyre sent me this picture from 1985:

The caption is a quote from Ronnie: "The Taliban Are The Moral Equivalent Of Our Founding Fathers." Really? I'll have to check to see if Jefferson banned kite flying for fear that someone would use a page from the constitution as a tail.

This shot of The Gipper witlessly schmoozing with these medieval mullahs says it all. We had no idea then, and we have no idea now, who is who over there and what we can possibly accomplish in a region where it's a hell of a lot easier to grow opium than democracy.

First, we sent a gaggle of CIA cowboys and psychopaths over to thumb our noses at the Russians-payback for all the noses they thumbed at us during Viet Nam. We delivered bags of cash and planeloads of sophisticated weapons to any warlord or jihadist who promised to point them at Ivan. It worked. One too many Stingers up the tailpipes of one too many Hind helicopters and Moscow took what was left of their toys and went home.

With no more bullies to torment, we got bored and ignored Afghanistan for the next fifteen years, until our former asset over there filled four airliners full of Saudi brethren with box cutters and made The War On Terror official.

We took out the Al Qaeda training camps with ship-based cruise missiles, taking zero casualties on our side. Ta! Da! The dawn of Global Unmanned Warfare.

And the more Unmanned and Unwomaned it gets, the more we replace G.I.'s with joysticks, the more children we remove from this Children's Crusade, the easier it is to keep this debacle a non-topic with the moms and dads and tax revolters at home.

Notice that all the drone and missile attacks on the cars and homes of the targeted locals are described as "surgical." As if there were this great medical practitioner, Dr. Counter Insurgency back in Washington, scanning the globe for cancers and surgically removing them with his Tomahawk and Hellfire scalpels.

If we can get away with printing fiat dollars forever, we can bring all the boys and all the girls home, and run the whole invisible show out of refrigerated control rooms, where young recruits, veterans of the point-and-shoot video culture put missiles between the eyes of every bozo marked with an "x" by the x-perts back at Langley, the Pentagon, Foggy Bottom or wherever those killers-at-a-distance are hiding out.

Author's note: Another audio play produced for Radio Free Oz at Dave Malony's Blue Ewe Studio on Whidbey Island, Washington. Script published on Bergman's Blog on September 21, 2010.

CHORUS:
(Sung to the tune of Mr. Sandman)
Dr. Blow Job, Send me a job
I'm out of work and I feel like a slob
Please twist on your Magic Knob,
And Dr. Blow Job send me, please, please mend me,
Dr. Blow Job, send me a job.

DR. B J: You're out of work and I'm not; and that's why I can show up to host the one program that puts Americans back to work, one American at a time. Our first job seeker is Steryl Gorgon of Brooklyn, Iowa.

STERYL: Happy to be on the show, Dr. Blow Job.

DR. B J: Call me, B. J., Steryl. So, where we're you pinked?

STERYL: At Midwest Great Pains Packing, Doctor. I was a standby safety chain saw operator at the lamb sluice.

DR. B J: That's hard work—but it's work. You stay right where you are Steryl…

STERYL: I've been doing that for months…

DR. B J: Our other job seeker is a first timer in the line. He's Tweed Eastern from Samesex, Massachusetts. Who was at the other end of your downsizing hatchet, Tweed?

TWEED: Worldwide Whatever. I was halfway through my training as a generic brands special events manager when the bubble burst.

DR. B J: Let's see if we can blow it up again.

MFX: THE HIRING THEME

DR. B J: The voice you're about to hear, because you can't see him behind the screen is a real employer with a real job opening.

SFX: AUDIENCE IS IMPRESSED

DR. B JJ: He'll test you each with a job related scenario and your solution to the problem will determine which of you will walk away with a job, and which will return to a life of uncertainty, restlessness and free floating stress.

STERYL: Sounds like you've been there.

THE BOSS: Mr. Gorgon, you're working for one of our communications divisions cutting a data pathway through an old growth redwood forest, and your blade accidently cuts through a nest of endangered songbirds. How would you alert the authorities?

STERYL: Well, sir, where I come from we have a saying, "Eat what you kill and have the EPA for desert.

SFX: APPRECIATIVE APPLAUSE

DR. B J: You come strong out of the box there, Steryl.

THE BOSS: Mr. Eastern, you're working as a tour-person in one of our theme parks and the fun bus you're on accidently runs over a trained pony at the petting zoo. How do you handle the shocked crowd of tourists and school children?

TWEED: I'd remind them, sir that it's a zero sum life now. When that pony goes into our meat wagon, it means more hamburger for everybody.

SFX: APPRECIATIVE APPLAUSE

Dr. B J: Let's eat! And now the moment of truth. Who gets hired and who stays mired? The moment of truth; and yet truth really doesn't have anything to do with it. If it did, the vast majority of the unemployed would be back at work and the handful of lazy, system-playing, out of work slakers would fall of the radar, or hire themselves out to GOP rallies as negative role models.

THE BOSS: I've made my decision. I don't want Steryl…

STEYRL: (SWEARS UNDER HIS BREATH)

THE BOSS: And I don't want Tweed…

TWEED: (REACTS POORLY)

THE BOSS: I want them both! I want Ruthless <u>and</u> Truthless!

SFX: WILD APPLAUSE

DR. B J: I know good news when I hear it.

STEYRL & TWEED: Thanks, Doc….etc.

CHORUS:
Dr. Blow Job, you got me a job
Now I can eat and I don't have to rob.
You turned on your Magic Knob
They downsized and pinked me;
You made them rethink me,
Dr. Blow Job, thanks for the job!

A NEW FACE ON ULTRA RIGHT WING MOUNTAIN

Bergman's Blog, September 23, 2010

How about that Christine O'Donnell? She has leapt out of a well-deserved obscurity and joined Sarah Palin, Sharron Angle and Michele Bachmann atop the Mt. Rushmore of ultra right wing ladies.

You might ask why Phyllis Schlafly, the demagogue of the Eagle Foundation isn't up there with them. After all, Texas replaced Thomas Jefferson with Phyllis in their school history curriculum, and that ought to get her already chiseled face chiseled up there with the other femme fatales of American fascism. But Phyllis is too old school and just doesn't have the requisite Q.

Not so, our gal Christine. She has vaulted up the steps of the temple of christian politics (I spell "christian" with a small "c" because there's not a drop of Christ in it) proudly waving all the buzzword banners of her reactionary cult. To Christine, homosexuality is an identity disorder, masturbation is adultery, AIDS victims have only themselves to blame, abortion is a crime even in cases of rape and incest and the U.S. is already mired in socialism.

When she ran for the Senate in 2006 she heard "the audible voice of God" who probably told her she was going to take a shellacking, but promised she would be carried to victory in 2010 by all the Delaware nut cases who feared His wrath should they fail to elect His anointed.

Divine intervention is one explanation for Christine's remarkable victory ; but there is another more ominous scenario.

When Chris was dating witches back in high school, doing the nasty on blood stained Satanic alters, did she make a pact with the darkest PAC of them all? Is Lucifer managing her run for the roses?

Is that why Karl Rove is so all over her? Does a whiff from O'Donnell's sulphurous campaign remind Karl of his old mentor, whose black arts served him so well in the White House? Is the Rovester jealous now that the Fly Master has chosen Christine's dung pile of smears and lies to hatch his eggs? Stay tuned. The soap opera has just begun.

GOP-THE CONSTIPATED CROCAGATOR
Bergman's Blog, September 24, 2010

There's an old saw that might explain it. A tourist traveling through central Louisiana stops at a general store to ask directions. The local behind the counter warns him to be on the lookout for crocagators, because they're the meanest critters around. "What's a crocagator," asks the tourist. "A crocagator," explains the local, " has the head of a croco-dile on one end and the head of an alligator on the other." "Really", exclaims the tourist. "How does it take a crap?" "That's why they so mean!" replies the local.

The GOP has morphed into a constipated crocagator, for sure.

On one end they're headed by the Tan Man in the House and Mitch The Bitch in the Sen-ate, who bitterly mourn the passing of the good old days of the Bush coup, and are tasked with little more than saying, "no."

On the other end, they're led by the know-nothing fatheads who yearn for the return of their bulging 401 k's, unlimited home equity and cradle-to-grave jobs. The Bushies mourn and the Teabaggers yearn but the crocagator monster can't take a good political crap.

Deep in its troubled heart, it knows the world it took for granted is slipping away, re-placed by a diorama of stable gay families, hard-working immigrants, sustainable off-the-gridders, a super smart, unflappable, Not-Me President and gaggles of over-night celebri-ties on the red carpet, wearing meat or nothing at all.

The GOP crocagator may wreck havoc in the midterms; but in the long term, it is, to quote another monster, "on the wrong side of history."

BANANA CLIP REPUBLIC
Ossman's Blog, September 24, 2010

down by the Borderline   a guy

wants a gun   a glock

goes out and gets one   a grip

on glory

fully loaded

       enough big shiny bullets inside to blast

       a platoon

       of toy soldiers   and reload

       on the undead

normal enough crazy guy   on the Borderline

buys bullets

easy as golf-balls

get it?   got it!   go!

now you

are the most armed and dangerous guy

in your

       Borderline barrio

       at the open-carry Safeway

       bulls-eye Kindergarten

       side-arm Sunday School

get it?   you got   a vision!

carries it out like that!

like Clint would

and would have gone on   gone on

       went on

          goes on

reloading

exploding like a coat full of nails

at a market in Kabul

a truckload of high-test fertilizer

outside a Starbucks

but for a slo-mo moment

when

        the reload

                      slipped his grip

EMPIRE JEOPARDY: RED CLOAK FOR BREAKFAST

Bergman's Blog, September 27, 2010

Author's note: Yet another fully produced audio play whipped up at Blue Ewe Studio. Dave Malony joins in as a cast member and producer.

YERRY: I'm Yerry Jerow, the host of America's world class Web game – EMPIRE JEOPARDY! This is the show that winds you up as the American Century winds down.

SFX: CROWD CHEERS

YERRY: Today's contestants. He's a Vertical Urban Farmer from Battered Washington. Meet Jack Browndart. How's it goin', Jack?

JACK: It's growin', Mr. Jerow. Up and up and up.

YERRY: He's the Commander of Former Intelligence at SINQCOM DREDSENT AFPAK in Hintville, Arkansas. Meet Lt. Col Buddah Brownschweig. Colonel, what <u>is</u> SINQCOM DREDSENT AFPAK?

BUDDAH: I wasn't in long enough to find out, Yerry.

YERRY: She's a Loan Denier for Windjammer-Gorgol in Jockeyshorts, Illinois. Meet Swindeloo Zimmer. Working hard, Swindeloo?

SWINDELOO: Saying "no" is becoming a real growth business, Mr. Jerrow.

YERRY: The rules are as simple as our contestants. Win two and we talk. Lose two and you walk. Tie and you try again next time. Here we go. "Two hundred and twenty-one million nine hundred and forty-three thousand, five hundred and sixty-seven."

SWINDELOO: What's a number large enough to confuse people?

SFX: "WRONG!" BUZZER

BUDDAH: What is the cost of a B-1 stealth fuselage?

SFX: " WRONG!" BUZZER

JACK: What is the number of barrels of crude oil the BP well has spilled into the Gulf as of an hour ago.

SFX: "RIGHT!" BELL

YERRY: One for you, Jack. I see you stay on top of things. Here we go again. "Hiding billions of dollars of debt by not selling what you don't want until you get it back."

SWINDELOO: What is "window dressing?"

SFX: "RIGHT!" BELL

YERRY: That was fast, Swindeloo.

SWINDELOO: Easy. I used to date one of the Lehman Brothers when I worked at B of A.

YERRY: We're down to it, now. Swindeloo and Jack, maybe we talk. Buddah Brownschweig, maybe you walk. Here it is. "Red Cloak For Breakfast."

JACK: What is the latest gluten-free diet?

SFX: "WRONG!" BUZZER

SWINDELOO: What is taking an early meeting with the Cardinal?

SFX: "WRONG!" BUZZER

BUDDAH: What is the Hopi symbol of the Cataclysmic Purification of America?

SFX: "RIGHT!" BELL

YERRY: Bingo!

BUDDAH: We talked about it all the time at SINQCOM.

YERRY: Well, you'll get to talk some more, Buddah, because you tied it up and you'll all be back next time on EMPIRE JEOPRADY.

APPLAUSE; THEME OUT.

OBAMA CARE-THE DOCTOR IS IN

Bergman's Blog, September 29, 2010

Polling on Obama Care has been pretty consistent, 40% like it, 40% don't like it and the other 20% could care less. That over half the public is unimpressed with this major reform of our health care system puzzles me; but what I find most astonishing is the insane lengths to which the opposition has gone to demonize it.

How about those Death Panels we would face, deciding if there's enough wage earner left in us to pay for the heart transplant? Totally bogus, but that doesn't stop Sister Sarah and her Foxy friends from spreading the lie, and scarring half our rest home residents to death. So, in the pursuit of truth and sanity, let's take a look at the key Obama Care reforms that went into effect last week.

First: Providers won't be able to cancel a policy because of a typo on the application. The insurance companies will have to find other work for the legion of nitpickers, who cast honest clients into purgatory for want of Spell Check.

Second: Insurers can't deny coverage to kids because of pre-existing conditions like hay fever, asthma, or sports injuries. I get it. Why should we make the kids suffer just because there's too much ragweed, polluted air and AYSO leagues?

Third: No more limits on the amount of coverage. So if I develop a chronic condition, I don't have to lose my life savings, my self-esteem and move back in with my parents in Shaker Heights.

Fourth: The provider will pay for mammograms and standard immunizations. Pretty radical, huh? Denying Americans their inalienable right to breast cancer, diphtheria, polio, mumps and measles.

Fifth: In case of a medical crisis, I can use the nearest emergency room without penalty. That's a relief. The last time I had a car accident, I had to drive my broken body in my broken car across town to my local ER to cover the charges.

There they are. The core of the new

regulations that health care providers must abide by. Not exactly the Maoist, Stalinist, communist, socialist, totalitarian take over that the corporate shills, co-opted congressmen and over-steeped Teabaggers are trumpeting.

Wait a minute! Are the Insurance Barons threatened by the prospect of healthy Americans? Do they fear that if they can no longer "play doctor" with our bodies, that we'll recover and take back the treasures they stole from our sick beds? Does that vision make them ill?

Not to worry. Their local Obama Care physician is in, and will see them now.

DONALD GNOME THE FIRST
BY DAVID OSSMAN

Of all the Garden Gnomes we've got
Donald trumps the lot!

His pointy hat he's combed straight back
To point up his steely brow.
His taste in gold is bold as brass, so
Gnome of the Moment, take your bow!

When more cement gets dumped
Inside the Donald mold
Donald claims the Gnomes are pumped
To buy, sell and be sold!

They're fired, Don, with Vegas schemes,
Viagra dreams that make their rowboats grow
Long and sleek - to muscle-yachts
With lots of busty blonds below.

Yes, first you skim the stupid out – Gnomes'll vote
For a familiar face forever.
Then gather round the Birther Gnomes,
They'll believe a TV star – whatever!

Now pluck the greedy gamblers up,
Some Mormon Gnomes mayhap,
Then – ooops! Your ratings, Don,
They're falling! Crap!

Off those Gnomes have gone, to look at someone new
Cause in our House of Garden Gnomes they'll find
More faithful, solid plaster Gnomes, red-white-and-blue.

And now that pointy-hatted Garden Guys
Are Governors of Garden-Gnomish States
And sit on plushy Senate seats,
Freshly painted, party ready with their mates,

Those cutesy Garden Gals, painted plaster to the core,
On lawns from Gnome Alaska to the plains of OklaGnoma,
They're frankly more seductive, Don, much more

Than you. So thanks a lot for April Fools, now back
To the B-list Gnomes you like to push around. You know,
A Garden Gnome on a Penthouse lawn
Don't make the garden grow.

Of all the Garden Gnomes we've got
Donald trumps the lot!

EMPIRE JEOPARDY: BILLION DOLLAR MAN
Bergman's Blog, September 30, 2010

YERRY: This is Yarry Jarrow and welcome to Empire Jeopardy, the Web's most popular game show and double dip of fun. I'm your host and witness as the Empire winds itself up and just keeps unwinding. All three contestants are back from last week. He's an urban vertical farmer from Battered, Washington, and winner of this year's *Golden Trellis Award*. Meet Jack Browndart. What's the *Golden Trellis*, Jack?

JACK: It's the Oscar of Vertical Permaculture, Yerry. I won it for growing 380 pounds of Brussels sprouts up the elevator shaft of an abandoned factory. I brought some for you.

YERRY: Thanks a bushel, Jack. He was the Commander of Former Intelligence at CINQCOM DREDSCENT AFPAC in Hintsville, Arkansas; but he's been picked to head the Unmanned Manpower Center at the Drone Alone Air Force Base on Growler Island, Washington. Meet Colonel Buddah Brownschweig. That's quite a promotion they gave you, Colonel.

BUDDAH: Once they heard about my Powerpoint they had to have me.

YERRY: She was a loan denier for Windjammer Gorgol on Jockeyshorts, Illinois until they kicked her upstairs to run the whole Loan Denial Division in their Tipping Point, Washington Headquarters. Meet Swindaloo Zimmer. Happy about the transfer, Swind-eloo?

SZ: Working for Windjammer Gorgol is the best life sentence in the business, Mr. Jarrow.

YERRY: The rules are as simple as our returning contestants. Win two and we talk, lose two and you walk, tie it up and we come back for more. Here we go. "Four Out Of Every Five."

JACK: What is the percentage of packaged foods that contain empty calories?

SFX: "WRONG!" BUZZER

BUDDAH: What is the percentage of civilians collateralized by a Predator launched Hellfire missle?

SFX: "WRONG!" BUZZER

SWINDELOO: What is the percentage of the unemployed turned away from every job opening?

SFX: "RIGHT!" BELL

YERRY: Right you are, Swindeloo!

SWINDELOO: A lot of them sleep outside my office.

YERRY: Let's go again. "They're Invisible, Hard To Catch and Worth One Hundred Billion Dollars."

JACK: What is left of the salmon in Alaska?

SFX: "WRONG!" BUZZER

SWINDELOO: Who are all the wealthy deadbeats who walked on their mortgages?

SFX: "WRONG!" BUZZER

BUDDAH: Who are the 100 AL Qaeda bums still operating in Afghanistan?

SFX: "RIGHT!" BELL

YERRY: Bingo, Buddah!

BUDDAH: If you can't find 'em, you can't drone 'em.

YERRY: So here we are. Swindaloo and Buddah, we could talk. John, you're one wrong answer away from walking.

JACK: Don't sell my Birkenstocks short, Yarry.

YERRY: Here it is. " A Clueless Barfly With Delusions Of Grandeur."

SWINDELOO: Who is John Boehmer?

SFX: "RIGHT!" BELL

YERRY: Right on, Swindeloo! It's John Boehmer, the Sultan of Suntan.

SWINDELOO: I speed dated him once. Five minutes was enough.

YERRY:And here's what you've won, Swindy. A million dollars worth of Goldman Sachs Of Crap toxic derivatives. They're perfect for wallpapering your nest egg. A complete set of The Presidents Heads In Chocolate from the Franklin After Dinner Mint; and an all expenses paid weekend on Louisiana's Gas War Island Resort. Slip into your Hawaiian Hazmat halter, order up a couple of 30 weight Mohitos on us and chill out. Talk about a private beach. You're the only living thing within 10 miles! This is Yarry Jerrow, Host of Empire Jeopardy reminding you that everybody else is just a failed attempt at being us.

THE MIDTERM ELECTIONS: A VIEW FROM THE BRINK

Bergman's Blog, September 30, 2010

I've been swimming against the current of public opinion in the Big River of Denial too long.

I have to climb out over its failed banks and towel off the illusion that the voting public will wake up from their long midterm nap and keep the relatively sane Democratic Party in control of Congress.

Hope may spring eternal; but those springs have been thoroughly evaporated by the extraordinary heat coming from the Right.

The combination of Super PAC's run by the likes of Karl Rove; suitcases of cash from billionaire bandits, who remain in the shadows thanks to the Bad Boys on the Supreme Court, and the drumbeat of fear and falsehood emanating from the lipstick liars and amoral alter boys on Fox is just too much for our fragile democracy to withstand.

It's happened before.

During the 30's, fascist clerics, hooded racists, armed vigilantes and King Fish dictators strove for the hearts and minds of Americans, mired in a decade long depression. Only World War II and the full employment that came in its wake saved them from that dark crowd.

No wartime prosperity can save us now.

It is, in fact, our endless war against the "terrorists", "insurgents", "militants" and locals who get in the way that has brought us to the brink of financial and moral bankruptcy.

Into this spiritual vacuum have stepped the know-nothings, nay-sayers, homophobes, xenophobes, ayatollahs, misogynists and seditionists, sidelined until now by a bubble economy and a corrupt empire.

I fear that nasty gang is going to have their way for a while; and perhaps a dose of their second-rate minds and third-rate solutions will sober us up.

Perhaps, those springs of hope will flow again, even if it takes the hard reign a comin' to fill them.

ON NOVEMBER 2ND, DO THE RIGHT THING

Bergman's Blog, October 4, 2010

These are confusing times, no doubt. In a little over a year we have seen our economy tank, our empire implode and our culture unravel.

Whether we've entered a bona fide "Big D" depression or are just double-dipping doesn't change the fact that half the states are bankrupt, real unemployment is nearly double what the government will admit and the specter of homelessness stalks millions of Americans who, until recently, were sleepwalking through the American dream.

We can't pump up the war machine because we lost the handle chasing vandals in and out of the Middle East; and the loyal opposition in Congress is loyal only to their simple-minded scheme of bringing down the government so they can root around for goodies in the ashes.

"These are the times that try men's souls", and we have been tried and found wanting on at least one count of spineless stupidity.

Both ends of the political spectrum have abjured any responsibility for the mess we're in and shifted the explanation to a series of self-serving conspiracy theories, all starring Barack Hussein Obama.

The Tea Party version has been grabbing column inches for months. Obama is a dedicated, anti-colonial, Kenyan anchor baby, sent here to take away our guns, our Hummers and our right to die from lack of proper health care.

The rants from the disgruntled left have the look of legitimate research; but in the end are just as farfetched.

My favorite is the screed that ties Obama's father and the rest of his family to a variety of CIA plots against good-guy African leaders, and then reveals the military/industrial cabal behind Barack's rise to the presidency. All that's missing are the Illuminati, The Elders Of Zion and The Spear Of Longinus.

Obama's not the Manchurian candidate. He's a remarkable person trying to clean up a White House befouled with eight years of sedition and greed. He got the Nobel Prize just for being elected! That's a measure of the doo-doo left behind by Dubya and the horse he rode out on.

Take another look at TARP-it worked. Study the Stimulus Bill-it's a transforming vision. And come November 2nd-get off your disgruntled ass and do the right thing.

CORPORATE AMERICA:
TURNING PINK INTO GOLD
Bergman's Blog, October 5, 2010

The Wall Street Journal says that Corporate America finished the second quarter of 2010 with "near-historic" profits. Now, there's a piece of economic legerdemain.

How do you make beaucoup bucks in the midst of The Great Depression Lite? Profits from the S&P 500 are up 38% from last year -- the sixth-highest quarterly total ever. It would be a good thing, if those behemoths had raked in all that scratch by selling a whole lot of widgets or servicing a ton of clients. No way. Since 2008, corporate revenues have shrunk 6 % while all those profits were being generated.

They did it by magic. Not black magic, but pink magic. Corporate America is making out like the moral bandit it is by firing people right and left and outsourcing every job it can possibly deport.

The nation is awash in pink.

The 77,000 job hires in September couldn't compensate for the final exit of the census takers (another ten years before that Stimulus returns) and the regular growth of the labor force; so, the unemployment upticks to 9.7.

Simultaneously, the Fed has hammered the prime rate down to 99 Cent Store proportions; so, the same companies handing out the pinks are borrowing oodles of green for next to nothing.

This country's mega businesses are hoarding $1.6 trillion of cash, while small businesses and households can't borrow a dime. Not a recipe for prosperity in any economic cookbook I've read.

It all comes down to the flow of capital, the lifeblood of our national economy. If Corporate America continues to squat on its cash instead of investing it in we the people; and if the Federal Government continues to squander our treasure abroad instead of investing it in we the people, then that lifeblood will not flow and our economy will go into shock.

We're all about turning the Federal Government upside down. Why not the corporations? They're only a legal fiction. The corporate veil can be pierced with the stroke of a pen. Make the Board of Directors and the major shareholders personally responsible for the careers they terminate and the jobs they smuggle abroad.

That just might put us back in the pink.

Corporate America's New Fall Line:
SACKCLOTH!
It's what the sacked and soon-to-be-sacked
will be wearing all across the country!

From playoffs to layoffs, this fall you'll
be wearing their new line and loving it!

A BEACON OF BURNING TANKERS

Bergman's Blog, October 9, 2010

The flaming hulks of NATO fuel trucks, stretching from the AfPak border to Islamabad cast a baleful light on the shadow war we have been waging in Pakistan.

Understand, the Taliban thugs who torched those tankers have the sympathy of every Pakistani whose lives are threatened daily by the rain of Hellfire missiles.

In the last month, the Pentagon and the CIA have more than doubled their Predator attacks over Pakistan. Their stated rationale? They need to beef up their Boogey Men body count before the White House does their reassessment of the whole AFPak adventure.

It's time we made our reassessment.

(1) What can we accomplish by putting boots on the ground and drones in the air in Pakistan? The Taliban and a broad range of other hard line, Islamist groups are standard fare in a country that was founded as a breakaway Islamic haven.

(2) What real help can we expect from the Pakistani army, government or security services? For decades, they have been using us, lying to us and supporting the warlords and jihadists who have been killing us.

(3) What have our incursions into Pakistan accomplished except to increase the risk of terrorist attacks against our homeland? The Times Square car bomber was provoked by our Predator strikes. He is not alone.

(4) What level of blood and treasure will we have to pour into Pakistan to make a difference? 100,000 troops and $2,000,000,000 a week isn't doing the job in Afghanistan.

(5) What's the end game? Will it take the head of Bin Laden, a feminist Taliban, an opium free Afghanistan and text book democracies from Baghdad to Baluchistan to satisfy us? Can't we just pack up The American Dream and come home?

If we answer these questions and choose to act, we have a shot at turning this madness around. If not; we can join the drones at home, follow our leaders and pay the parking meters. Buddy, can you spare a dime?

NO TOM PAINE, NO GAIN

Bergman's Blog, October 13, 2010

As I drove off the ferry onto the mainland recently I read an election sign that accused the local Democratic congressman of "Bankrupting The Country since 1992." I'm getting whiffs of 1932 and "1984" here.

1932-"Bankrupting The Country Since 1992" -- read, "We're in this mess because they stabbed us in the back." Hitler did a great job of convincing an angry and dispirited German people that all their problems lay at the feet of the Not-Me. It was the Jews and Commies in '32. It's Obama and the liberals today.

"1984"-The barrage of lies and slander coming out of the right wing media maw is Orwellian in proportion. Thanks to a reactionary majority on the Supreme Court, secret money from anywhere -- inside and outside the country -- is pouring into the campaign, doled out by the likes of the Koch brothers and Satan's little helpmate, Karl Rove.

Six months ago, when the Tea Party was beginning to steep and the Republican far right was beginning to draw blood from the President, I called up my reserve of American optimism and figured that the peoples' common sense would come to the defense of our democracy. It didn't.

Goebbels was right. I was wrong. In a time of desperate confusion and economic collapse -- 30's Germany in the throes of the Great Depression and present day America in the grip of the Double Dip -- it would take a nation of Philosopher Kings to accept their share of responsibility for the disaster and devise a reasonable plan for healing the Commonwealth.

We have been so numbed and weakened by our addiction to trash TV, empty calories and bogus credit that, as it stands, we are incapable of standing up to the anti-democratic forces co-opting our economy, our ecology, our foreign policy and our civil liberties.

We are being occupied by hostile forces, just as certainly as the 13 colonies were occupied by the British. We need a Second American Revolution to free ourselves.

Instead of a Tea Party -- a TV Party. Unhook our flat screens and let Glenn and Sarah and Sean stumble in the darkness.

Turn away from the Happy Meals of the undead and cook ourselves up a local, farm-fresh future.

Take a look at that hand of credit cards we've dealt ourselves. How long are we going to stay in the toilet, pulling for a flush?

We don't have to wait for Nov. 2nd to wake up. Obama is a truly decent man with the patience and humility of our first president. Speak up for him. Speak up for the vision of America he has risked his political future to create and defend.

We are the people. We can do it. Well-educated, well-fed and well-intentioned, we can take this country back from the forces of ignorance and greed. Remember, no Tom Paine – no gain.

THE GRAY AND THE BROWN-
THE NEW CIVIL WAR

Bergman's Blog, October 14, 2010

"The United States may be heading for an intensifying confrontation between the gray and the brown," says author Ronald Brownstein. Yes, as we trip into the Double Dip, older white folks are being replaced by brown and black kids; and, in a decade or so, young non-whites will be the national majority.

In response, older white folks have gone just, plain crazy. It's the simplest explanation for the mania that has gripped a vast segment of the over fifty, white Boomers. They are being simultaneously overwhelmed by the Not-Me and the Not-It.

The Not-Me is every member of the legion of young people of color-any color, any shade-that increasingly dominates the popular culture.

The Not-It is the new reality of disappearing jobs, evaporating credit and diminishing resources that overnight replaced their familiar world of American Exceptionalism.

Look at the crew of white seniors-to-be, leading the reactionary charge against anyone who smells like the Not-Me and anything that smacks of the Not-It. There's Rush Limbaugh, morphing daily into an even more poisonous windbag; the self-annointed Glenn Beck, calling on God Almighty to strike down his ever-growing enemies list and Laura Schlesinger who vomits up the "N" word when a woman of color has the temerity to call her show.

Who's listening to these pious pus-bags? The overwhelmingly white and over fifty Tea Party for sure, and 71% of Republicans identify with the Tea Party. It's the revenge of the getting-old people.

That's why back in January the entire GOP congressional delegation locked arms and brayed "Ney" at every piece of Democratic legislation. It's a form of magical thinking. Say "Ney" long enough and the problem will go away. But it won't.

If the super-rich and the super-pissed orchestrate a midterm bloodbath, and send a gang of know-nothing yahoos to Congress, who blame sun spots for global warming, American Muslims for Al Qaeda and masturbation for the decline of family values, things will get really bad, really soon.

States will go belly up, the infrastructure will crumble, unemployment will skyrocket, and the dream of the return of that "Shining Gated City On the Hill" will fade away. The angry grays will have to step aside and let a younger, multi-hued America put this country back on the road to recovery.

PUT GLENN IN THE CHILEAN MINE

Bergman's Blog, October 17, 2010

There they stood, hoses in hand, the brave firefighters of Obion County, Tennessee, instructed by their boss to let Gene and Paulette Cranicks' home burn to the ground, taking the family's dogs and cats with it. All because of a $75 fee that had been overlooked. Gene Cranick pleaded with the firemen, offered up the money, then tried to put out the blaze himself.

His reward, a thorough tongue lashing from that beady eyed marshmallow, Glenn Beck, who excoriated Cranick for trying to "sponge off his neighbors." In the background, Glenn's radio show side kick mocked Cranick's futile attempt to save his home and his pets.

If Don Imus deserves to be suspended for his thoughtless, racial slurs, then Beck has earned a place in the tunnel recently exited by the Chilean miners, to contemplate the darkness of his heart.

Beck's twisted response to the tragedy is no surprise. But he has been joined in the blogosphere and on the airwaves by a chorus of self righteous reactionaries and compassion free libertarians who display the spectre of the Cranicks' smoking ruins as a warning to every citizen who thinks they can get away with sucking off the American Dream.

Are these troubled times tearing us apart? Are we so spooked by the overnight disappearance of the Unlimited Everything that we'll let a neighbor's house burn and his pets fry because of a late fee? Do Glenn Beck and his morally bankrupt minions have their fingers on the true pulse of this nation, a pulse so amped with fear that we are unable to reach out and save our brothers and sisters in distress?

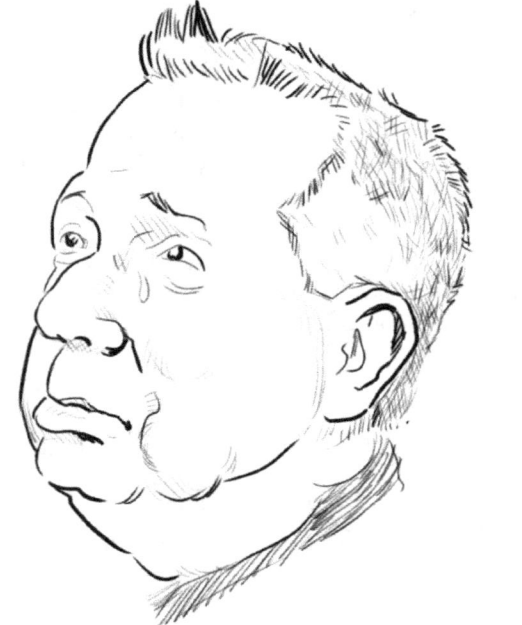

a

I don't think so. It's only matter of time before we come out of shock, find our center and put this nation back on its feet. As for Glenn and his ilk, the doggies and kitties whose fiery death they mocked, wait for them at the Gates Of Hell.

REDO THE MATH

Bergman's Blog, October 19, 2010

Let's do the math:

- We're down 11.5 million jobs since 2008 and won't replace them for twenty years.
- Official unemployment is hovering around 10% and actual unemployment is closer to 18%.
- Municipalities and states, perched on bankruptcy, are shedding cradle-to-grave jobs.
- The infrastructure is crumbling, the public school system is in crisis, and foreclosures are at an all-time high.
- Corporate America has chosen to sit on 1.5 trillion dollars in cash rather than invest in our economy.
- Just think what two billion dollars a week would do to change the math. Two billion dollars, that's what we're spending every week in Afghanistan.

It might be worth the sacrifice if two billion a week were bringing democracy with all its bells and whistles to Afghanistan, suppressing its heroin trade and securing the country from the local jihadists who stone women and behead villagers to satisfy their thirst for power and sexual domination.

It isn't buying any of that. Proof positive is the recent admission by our Secretaries of State and Defense that the U.S. is facilitating talks between the Taliban and what's left of Karzai's government. Our nine-year occupation of Afghanistan has been a failure. All that blood and treasure for nothing.

When we leave Afghanistan and sneak back home, that country will be a lot worse off than when we charged in post-9/11. Back then, the Taliban were contained in the Kandahar region by Masoud's Northern Alliance and a relatively stable regime in Kabul. Now those vicious freaks are everywhere. What we'll leave behind is anarchy, the same gift we're leaving behind in Iraq.

And we'll come home to anarchy. Where are we going to find jobs for a hundred thousand shell-shocked G.I.s? What have we got here for the other hundred thousand contract mercenaries to guard?

The empire is collapsing simply because we can't afford it. So, we redo the math.

We beat our swords into solar panels and do a hell of a lot more with a hell of a lot less.

We learn to live with the reality that other cultures aren't a failed attempt at being us; and we get straight with the fact that nation-building begins at home.

A HOOT TO BOOT

Bergman's Blog, October 21, 2010

This is a scary election, but it's also a lot of weird fun. I keep reminding myself how much is at stake and then whammo! there's Rand Paul sparking up a college girl-friend, blindfolding her and taking her down to the river to bow before The Aqua Buddha. Come on, it doesn't get any kookier than this.

How about Christine O'Donnell, another stellar Republican senatorial candidate, who did the nasty on a bloodstained, satanic altar as a teenager? This is good stuff.

Then there's Sharron Angle, the GOP wannabe senator who tells an auditorium of high school Hispanics that they look like Asians to her. I'd have trouble making that up.

Let's not forget Ron Johnson, the cheese-head running against Russ Feingold, who con-fronts record world temperatures and sees sun spots.

Or Carl Paladino, the homophobic gubernatorial candidate who runs the hottest gay clubs in Buffalo.

Or Joe Miller up in Alaska, who cuffs reporters when they get too close. These guys are a gift to anyone with a sense of humor.

We will remember this midterm election as the final revenge of the crazy, old white people. We will mark it as the final stage of the unraveling of the once-noble party of Abraham Lincoln.

We will look back at the two years of partisan gridlock and know-nothing fingerpointing that this election ushered in as the springboard to The New New Deal -- the multi-ethnic, multi-aged, super-smart, totally practical solution to the economic and spiritual catastro-phe that Bush and his corrupt gang of powermongers, bean counters and war lovers have bequeathed us.

Yes, Dear Friends, this midterm election is all that and a total hoot to boot.

YOUR TICKET TO BUNKER HILL

Bergman's Blog, October 28, 2010

I just read that the top 74 wage earners in this country made as much in 2009 as the 19 million, lowest-paid American workers.

Why don't we start our own Tea Party around that?

These are Tea Party Times.

Boston was occupied by the British.

We're occupied by Corporate America and the Super-rich.

England occupied America to protect a major market.

Corporate America occupies this country to protect the market it's rigged for the last seventy-five years.

What's today's metaphor for the bales of tea that the "Mohawks" threw into the Bay in 1773?

How about the Corporate American life style?

Can we dress up like capable human beings instead of post-apocalyptic plague dandies, walk over to the brink and toss that corrupt and unsustainable life style overboard?

Say, "Yes" to that, and we can meet up on Bunker Hill.

MY MIDTERM NIGHTMARE

By Peter Bergman, Election Eve, 2010

This piece is fashioned after The Nightmare Song from Gilbert & Sullivan's operetta "Iolanthe."

I am lying awake with a midterm headache, my psyche is wracked with anxiety.

I am badly confused and feel terribly used by the fat cats who run our society.

I'm anxious and frightened, my terror is heightened by the news that comes out of Fox Cable;

All pompous and smiley, that bastard O'Reilly spouts off from his tower of Babel.

I'm brimming with dread from each prim talking head, I can't even look at Sean Hannity

He's all certain and sure as he spreads his manure; I well could be losing my sanity.

So, I fall off to sleep in the wake of that creep and his legion of logical errors;

And the dreams that I dream of the Dems getting creamed are beset with electoral terrors.

I see myself flying in space and I'm eyeing my countrymen making decisions;

From the West to the East, from the most to the least it's a picture of rents and divisions.

There is want, there is waste and a lack of good taste, all is calumny, cant and profanities;

The pictures and scenes on the zines and the screens are an incessant stew of inanities.

In Alaska, Murkowski may soon lose her house key to the ladies room back at the Senate;

The Tea Party anger will probably hang her like it did back in Utah to Bennett.

Jerry Brown's using Whitman's own words as his hit-man, the Moonbeam out thought and outfoxed her.

In the Senate arena is Carly Fiorina and a heavyweight champion Boxer.

McCain and Jan Brewer (no sane man would screw her) are getting that dang fence erected.

They talk law and order, but down at the border, the visitors pass undetected.

Harry Reid's in a tangle with Ms. Sharon Angle, the queen of press conference evasion;

Who states without panic to a school of Hispanics, that somehow they all seem so Asian.

The millionaire, Johnson who's up in Wisconsin giving Feingold a regular whipping,

Says he thinks global warming is sunspots performing-hey, dude, I've just got to be tripping!

Paladino, the porker wants to govern New Yorkers, campaigning from upstate to Zabars,

When he's not cursing homos, or losing to Cuomo, he runs Buffalo's two hottest gay bars.

There's Christine the witch-the Tea Party Bitch-the first to take moral offendment

Who was stunned and irate when she learned church and state were cut loose in the premiere amendment.

And then, last of all there's the son of Ron Paul tryin' out as a good Christian liver;

Since the story that broke of the girl he got stoked and made bow down to God in the river.

I wake up at last, the nightmare had passed, and there's light streaming in through the curtain,

In the clear glow of dawn, I feel hope coming on, and of one thing I know I am certain.

We've come out of a bubble in serious trouble, the goo in the Gulf's killing fishes.

The money is horded, all All Main Street is boarded; the vibe in the hood's getting vicious.

If we don't fight for health, teach our kids, spread the wealth, we're all going to drown in this drama.

Just remember, my friends, as the darkness descends, we've got 2012 and Obama.

GAMEDAY FOR AMERICA

Bergman's Blog, November 2, 2010

Republican control of the House will do nothing but exacerbate the economic crisis that's engulfing us.

The House GOP leadership – if you can in your wildest dreams call John Boehner a leader -- comes to power with a plan to do little more than relentlessly investigate and harass the Obama administration, dismantle health care, extend tax cuts for the Super-rich and deregulate Corporate America.

This reactionary crusade isn't the carefully thought-out program of a Republican brain trust. Those know-nothings are suspicious of anyone with a brain, and have done nothing to earn our trust.

If there is a mind behind what is now called the GOP, it resides inches above the jowly puss of Karl Rove.

You are looking into the face of the new Rasputin – the most powerful politician on the right. And he has no politics!

He doesn't give a fig about abortion on demand, school prayer, gay marriage or Obama's birth certificate, and he has nothing but contempt for those who do.

He is interested in power – nothing more. He had power over George W. Bush and this nation once, and has returned to take that power back as the ruthless front man for the financial and corporate elite.

He and everyone he represents stand in the way of an equitable recovery for all Americans.

Know your enemy, and know the power that energizes this moral zombie. It is the ultra-moneyed class that dictates to our corporations, rigs our financial markets and buys every politician up for sale.

The election is over and the game has begun. They're the rich school with all the fancy equipment. Their mascot is Karl Rove – a pig in a jacket.

We're the poor school, and we're playing them on their anything-but-level playing field. Our mascot is Barack Obama – a mensch in a pickle.

Let's go cream their asses and take back our country – the trophy they're holding hostage.

PICKING THE (GRID)LOCK

Bergman's Blog, November 3, 2010

I hate gridlock! When I lived in Los Angeles I learned all the shortcuts around the traditional traffic jams; but once in a while I would be caught in a pile up and sit there fuming, taking it personally.

Now I have at least two years of gridlock to look forward to in Washington D.C. Totally unacceptable, but what in the world can I do about it?

Gridlocked in traffic I have fantasized leaving my car in the jam and walking away. Can I just walk away from politics until the jam is cleared? I won't; but, I think a lot of Americans are going to tune out as the likes of John Boehner, Mitch Cantor and Darrell Issa try to tear down everything Obama and the Democrats have accomplished over the past two years.

There couldn't be a worse time in our history to lapse into a period of contentious, do nothing gridlock. We are in the first stages of a major depression, and need all the stimulus we can pump into our collapsed economic veins.

I see this playing out one of two ways:

- We are so bitter, confused, frustrated and overwhelmed that we give up struggling and let Karl Rove and his posse of demons take control. It's the road to fascism and it's not lined with good intentions, but with no intentions at all.
- We pick ourselves up, climb out of the emotional and financial hole we've helped dig and confront the Corporate American lifestyle and the power-mad plutocrats on every front.

Now, there's a choice, for you. One doesn't take any energy at all. Let the bastards have their way, and we'll get by on the scraps that trickle down from their Gated City On The Hill.

The alternative is a call to total action. We have the wherewithal to force the change; it resides in the simple choices we make every day.

Every time we choose the Commonwealth over wealth alone; every time we choose to live more fully with less, and every time we act as interdependent neighbors and citizens instead of antagonists in a zero sum game we move one step closer to renewing this great country.

I choose to stay in the trenches, because I don't like what's waiting out there in No-Man's Land.

JOBS JOBS JOBS

Bergman's Blog, September 8, 2010

What's all this talk about structural unemployment. There's work out there, you just have to know where to find it. Here are four fabulous gridlock-proof fields of opportunity.

ROBO-SIGNER: Have you got a strong wrist and little moral curiosity? There are stacks of foreclosure documents waiting for your John Hancock. You don't have to read what you're signing, and there's a bling bonus if you beat the quota.

NAY-SAYER: The Republicans have done a non-stop job of braying "nay" to everything Democrats have come up with to deal with the double dip we've been dealt. Boehner and his bad brothers are hoarse from two years of being horses' asses, and need a break. So, if you know how to say "no" load and clear to any plan that's remotely useful to our present dilema, then shuffle off to D.C. and get to work.

HUMAN FENCE: Everyday, hordes of illegal immigrants are pouring into the country across our porous border to the south. Here's a chance to put yourself and your country back to work. Link hands with millions of your fellow unemployed and make a fence of flesh, denying access to those who would infiltrate our economy, filling the very jobs that real Americans won't take because nobody plays them on television.

COUCH MINER: You can change your life with the smallest change, and that's what waiting for you, hidden in sofas and stuffed seats everywhere. Yes, it's time to leave the couch potato lifestyle behind; but, before you do, reach under the cushions of that couch and excavate those pennies, nickels, dimes and even quarters that are going to grubstake your return to reality. As you move up in life, you'll be sitting on fancier couches in fancier places and digging out the really big dough.

Get going now. You don't have time to wait around to find out if you're an anchor baby.

HOME IN AMERICA, NOVEMBER 2010

Ossman's Blog, November 12, 2010

Some of you may have heard an earlier, notebook draft of this poem a few days ago. This is the final version. -D.O.

Goodbye, America

home of the muscle car

home of the gun

Goodbye, America

home to dismemberment:

see Saw 3D and Postal 2 too

Home of the full-body scan

yet home to secret money

that buys the faithful's fears

America, bigots ran you for years

the once-upon-a-time Princes

got born, shot and died

The Colonels and Pop-Stars

tried to run you

but the Gun-Makers won

So the Spies ran you for the Billionaires

and by (Iowa) golly! Billionaires let

the Nobodies take over

So Nobody runs you now

Goodbye, America

home of the muscle car

home of the gun

Goodbye, America

home to dismemberment:

see Saw 3D and Postal 2 too

Home of the full-body scan

yet home to secret money

that buys the faithful's fears

America, bigots ran you for years

the once-upon-a-time Princes

got born, shot and died

The Colonels and Pop-Stars

tried to run you

but the Gun-Makers won

So the Spies ran you for the Billionaires

and by (Iowa) golly! Billionaires let

the Nobodies take over

So Nobody runs you now

and the muscle-car Nation

blows a valve

Dismembers the drive-shaft

flattens the tires, closes the schools

goes postal with prisons

Drives home on the rims

has a drink

and sits in the car til we're dead

We being America, goodbye

WHY SANTA'S BAG IS STUFFED WITH COAL

Bergman's Blog, November 22, 2010

Ben Bernanke, the Chairman of the Federal Reserve, has seen the light. He gets the fact that as important as stabilizing the deficit in the long run might be, pump-priming the economy in the short term -- and that means now -- is our primary and overriding priority.

For ever so long, Ben and the rest of the financial Wise Guys were guided by "the light at the end of the tunnel" leading us out of The Great Recession back to The Promised Land. That light has dimmed considerably of late, prompting Ben to take off his rose-colored specs and gaze across the grim economic landscape that stretches before us.

What does Ben say?

"On its current economic trajectory, the United States runs the risk of seeing millions of workers unemployed or underemployed for years. As a society, we should find that outcome unacceptable."

Forget "should," Ben. We must, from the very depths of our immortal souls. find that outcome morally repugnant and demand that it be rectified.

But it won't be easy, because the heartless hordes are gathering in Washington. Back in August, budget buffoon Stan Collender warned Bernanke that the GOP sees "economic hardship as the path to election glory." Those bastards want to bring Obama down on the backs of the working poor and unemployed.

The Democratic House has been no help. They just let unemployment benefits run out for two million more Americans. Those folks won't have the moolah to make hay in the malls. Black Friday, Ben, is turning a paler shade of gray.

Feels like we're back in Dickens' days, when naughty children found lumps of coal instead of sugarplums in their holiday stockings. That's how the compassion-free Republican ideologues are treating us: like bad boys and girls who have to be punished for having our lives blown apart when the bubble burst.

Lumps of coal, Ben. That's not the way we planned to get back into the black.

JOE'S GAVEL COULD DO THE JOB
Bergman's Blog, December 20, 2010

It's a brand new year, and soon we'll have a brand new Senate -- the 112th, to be exact. It's going to contain a lot fewer Democrats and some first-time world class wingnuts, like the global warming denier from Wisconsin and the Aqua Velva Buddha from Tennessee, but with any luck, the 112th may make history on its first day by doing away with the filibuster as we know it.

For the last two years, the Republican minority in the Senate has successfully stopped any and all legislation initiated by the Democrats by denying the body the sixty votes necessary to end a filibuster. It's nothing short of minority rule, and the GOP naysayers have done a fabulous job of using that tool to stop everything in its tracks, with the exception of a few pieces of legislation that were overwhelmingly popular, like their recent ending of Don't Ask Don't Tell.

Never in the history of our government, and as far as I can tell, in the history of any modern government, has the minority closed ranks and voted "no" on every piece of legislation put forward by the majority party.

Newt Gingrich shut down the government once and has threatened to help do it again, but who needs crazy Newt when the sixty-vote filibuster rule accomplishes the same goal.

It used to take sixty-seven votes to end a filibuster and force an up-and-down vote, until Robert Byrd changed that to sixty in 1975. At the time, Byrd said fifty-one Senators could change it again under the right conditions. Those conditions will apply January 5th, when the Senate reconvenes under the gavel of Vice President Joe Biden. Biden has let it be known that he's up for changing the rules so that a simple majority of fifty-one votes will end debate.

Tom Harkin, the veteran liberal, will be leading the charge, and if the Blue Dogs don't gum up the works, we could actually get the majority-rule government that our Founding Fathers and Mothers had in mind.

It won't necessarily change any of our long-standing problems -- chronic unemployment, outrageous income inequality, doomed imperial adventures and a crumbling infrastructure -- but it will prevent Mitch McConnell's claque of reactionary drones from holding the Senate hostage.

THE FOX NEWS FREAK SHOW

Bergman's Blog, December 21, 2010

Now we learn that people who watch Fox News are more likely to be misinformed than people who don't watch any TV at all, and that scary fact applies equally to self-identified Republicans and Democrats.

I don't watch a lot of Fox News. It's too hard on my brain and digestion. But only a brief sojourn in the land of "Fair and Balanced" is enough to explain why the poor souls who watch it are so confused and filled with fable instead of fact.

It's non-stop, lizard-brain-level entertainment disguised as news.

If all TV news has joined the circus, then Fox is the freak show outside the big tent, where the likes of O'Reilly, Hannity, Huckabee, Palin and Beck mesmerize the suckers and the rubes with sleazy tales of Obamacare death squads, two-hundred-million-dollar-a-day presidential trips to India, anchor baby terrorists and the secret agenda of American Muslims.

And like any good sideshow attraction, they're loud and rude, bullying their guests, wrapping themselves in phony piety, fretting over national security and questioning the patriotism of anyone who has the gall to question the latest slander they're passing off as fact.

So, why don't the people watching see through these bozos? The answer is, they'd rather be entertained than informed.

A substantial number of Americans have given up on the system thanks to the marvelous job the right wing has done over the last three decades denigrating our government and anyone connected with it, regardless of how qualified, hard-working and honest they might be.

Americans have been manipulated into an anti-government cynicism that despises parties, politicians and bureaucrats alike. So, why not veg out in front of your flat screen and let Murdoch's myrmidons feed your prejudices and stoke your anger?

And who benefits? The rich and powerful who thrive off a sedentary and suspicious electorate is who. They prosper off the hopelessness of others, always fearing that the American people will wake up some day out of their Fox-induced haze and put things right in this country.

Will it happen? The chances are remote, but the first step in claiming our freedom is pressing the "off" button on the remote we're holding in our hands.

HERE COME THE BOOBOISIE

Bergman's Blog, December 23, 2010

It won't be long before the eager crowds of Tea Baggers, young-earthers, global warming deniers, militiamen and compassion-free libertarians ride into Washington on the wave of free-floating, misdirected, national anger that sent them to the Capitol to do their worst.

For someone like me, who takes infinite pleasure chronicling the antics of the Booboisie, the next two years are going to be a hoot. I confess there's a tiny part of my psyche that wishes Christine O'Donnell, Sharon Angle, Tom Tancredo, Joe Miller and Rich Iott had made the cut.

Think how much livelier the 112th Congress would be with a teenage Satanist, a woman who turns unwanted pregnancies into lemonade, a world-class bigot, a man who handcuffs annoying reporters and a guy who likes to hang out on the weekends in an SS uniform roaming the halls of the House and the Senate.

It's no surprise that we elected such a bevy of over-the-top wingnuts to preside over us. They are us.

Look around. America has never been so over-the-top.

We weigh more pounds, watch more TV, wear more clothes, wave more fingers, whip more whipping boys, wave more flags, weave more conspiracies, wrestle more demons and want more of everything than ever before in our two-hundred-and-fifty-year history.

The next two years will tell the tale. Perhaps the gaggle of newly elected yahoos and know-nothings, inspired by the spirits of Washington, Lincoln and the Not-Me in the White House, will grow into their jobs.

Perhaps John Boehner will get even more deeply in touch with his feelings and reach out to the millions who need their government's help.

But I doubt it. I think we're in for two years of serve the rich and let God sort out the rest.

That's what we get for living in an over-the-top culture. The ultra-rich get ultra-richer, the middle class is marginalized, and the Booboisie dance in the halls of Congress.

DON'T LET SCROOGE FALL OFF THE WAGON

Bergman's Blog, December 24, 2010

It's the holiday season and I'm up early, cup of steaming java in my hand, perusing the front page of the newspaper. Stories of good will and cheer abound; Christmas dinners doled out to the homeless at the downtown mission, Marines collecting toys for tots and the needy delighted to find a basket of groceries delivered to their doorstep.

But on the same front page, there's another story devoid of all good will and cheer-it's the tale of the Republican legislative agenda for 2011. It's like Scrooge woke up on New Years Day and decided to revert to his mean spirited, miserly old ways.

The GOP, by their own account, are dead set on scuttling healthcare, education, highway and bridge repair, scientific research and nutrition for the poor. They are also determined to deep six the financial regulations put in place to prevent a repeat of the 2008 collapse which dragged us down into this Big Double Dip.

We're going to be hearing a lot about reigning in the deficit in 2011. Turning a blind eye to the vast sums we're spending on hapless military adventures across the globe, the Republicans (and way too many Democrats) are hell bent on staunching the flow of red ink by cutting back the very programs vital to our recovery.

We're building schools in Afghanistan while our own education system is on life support. We're paying for firefights in Kandahar, and can't afford to pay for firefighters at home. We're bulldozing superhighways from Kabul to Karachi, while our infrastructure is crumbling. Doesn't anybody get the irony here?

Yes, peace on earth and good will toward men; but first, peace here in America instead of class war and good will toward all the inhabitants of this marvelous country, rich and poor alike. Merry Christmas everybody, and a happy, hopeful new year.

DRAFTED INTO THE ARMY OF THE UNEMPLOYED

Bergman's Blog, January 8, 2011

On the front page of a recent USA Today is a ten-year chart displaying the percentage of unemployed Americans who have been jobless 27 or more weeks in the month of December.

The figures stand in stark contrast to the "Recovery Chorus" of pundits and financial gurus who would be blind by now for all the light they see at the end of the tunnel, were if not for the rose colored glasses surgically attached to their complacent faces.

The figures are disturbing. From a low of 11% in 2001, the figure moves inexorably up to 42% by 2010. Take that in. By the end of last year, half the unemployed have been out of a job for at least six months. Doesn't should like a recovery to me, more like a structural disaster.

And this is bad news that feeds on itself. Everyday you're out of work lessens your chances of finding another job. You lose skills, you lose touch with the latest tools, you lose your networks and you lose credibility with companies who would rather hire people who already have a job than someone carrying the stigma of being canned.

2011 is going to see more and more of our capable, hard working brothers and sisters drafted into the Army Of The Unemployed. Unlike the army that's wasting two billion bucks a week in Afghanistan, the Army Of The Unemployed gets little or nothing from the government, and when it does, it takes bribing the super rich and their pimps in Congress to eke out a few extra weeks of relief.

The prospects for a political solution are grim. Not only have we elected a House controlled by heartless prigs and ignorant yahoos, we are creating a class of permanently unemployed, who, like the poor are less likely to vote. The more time you spend scraping out an existence, the less time you have for politics.

So, what's it going to take to turn around this second Great Depression in our country's history? Popular wisdom credits the New Deal with pulling us out of the Big One in the 30's; but it took World War II to do that. Believe it or not, there's more pump priming in the Stimulus Bill that Barack and Joe dreamed up than in all the New Deal programs put together; but it will be two to three years before we really feel the effects. In the meantime, the super rich are going to get super richer, the middle class will continue to fade and the underclass will become an even more permanent sector of our beleaguered economy.

And there's no World War II to pull us out of this one. On the contrary, it's the feckless War On Terror that has sucked away all our treasure that didn't evaporate with the criminally engineered real estate credit bubble.

The only way we're going to get out of this Great Depression is from the grassroots up.

THE NEW NEW DEAL: TAX POLICY
Bergman's Blog, January 9, 2011

In my previous post I promised to outline my plan for digging ourselves out of this Big Double Dipper. I call my vision the New New Deal because what we are experiencing now hearkens to the Great Depression of the 1930s, bringing to mind the bold ideas and programs that FDR used to do battle with the economic chaos that was crippling the country.

Eight decades later, much has changed. We have tools and skills available to us today that were unimaginable in the '30s -- a nation connected by the Web, the miracles of modern medicine, accessibility of higher education. and major advances in racial, gender and sexual relations, just to name a few.

Yet in some ways, the '30s were better equipped to deal with the ravages of mass unemployment and poverty than we are today. The rural family farm and the urban nuclear family were the norm. They were able to absorb those extended family members who had lost their jobs or the wherewithal to survive.

Most of those family farms have been plowed under by agribusiness, and more than half the households today are managed by single parents. The social safety net of the '30s has been shredded; you can't go home again because there's nowhere to go.

Local, state and national governments have stepped in with their own safety nets, but the concept of government aid has never gone down easily in this country because we still cling to the endlessly propagated myth that America owes its greatness to the "rugged individual," whoever that is.

The fact that this romance bears little similarity to the dynamics of our immensely complicated, interdependent society hardly prevents Tea Party ideologues and right-wing media moguls from blowing long and hard about the plague of "welfare cheaters" and the apocalyptic perils of "Obama Socialism."

We're drowning in compassion-free propaganda. It's time we came up for air and reinvented the promise of this promised land.

So, here's the first area addressed by my New New Deal plan: Tax Policy

TAX EXCESSIVE, SPECULATIVE AND UNPRODUCTIVE WEALTH

What you tax and how much you tax it is a political, not moral, issue. There's nothing immoral about giving the super-rich another tax break. It might be fiscally reckless, but it's not immoral.

At what point is wealth excessive? I don't have an exact figure in mind, but around half a mil in annual salary and bonuses seems a reasonable tipping point. Tax 50 percent of earnings at that level, and ratchet up the rate as the earnings enter the arena of the obscene -- like the multimillions some CEOs are pulling in. Will they still stay on the job if they have to give back a serious slice of their super-salaries and mega-bonuses? If they ankle the job, there are plenty of qualified suits waiting in the wings to fill that vacant seat in the spacious corner office or on the corporate jet.

Then there are speculative earnings, like all the money being made at the speed of light on the stock market. The average trade on the market today lasts 18 seconds. It's nothing but gambling and deserves to be taxed accordingly. I think 95 percent is a fair rate. The Wall Street hot shots can gamble 24/7 if they please and take home a nickel for every buck they suck out of the system.

Unproductive wealth must also be rigorously taxed. Corporations and the super-rich are hoarding trillions of dollars, much of which belongs back in the system instead of salted away in off-shore banks. Hoarding reduces the velocity of capital, one of the key components of our economy's health. Either they invest the money in productive enterprises or we tax a substantial part and put it to work putting people back to work.

Soon I will outline the New New Deal's Education Policy. It's all about standing up to all this dumbing down.

MARSHMALLOWS & DESPAIR

Ossman's Blog, January 10, 2011

Yes, that's the title for my new and growing collection of "political" poems. Here's where the title comes from: Sam Sifton, a NYTimes restaurant critic wrote " . . . an America we all wish we lived in, where the pigs are fat and healthy instead of lean and terrifying, and yams taste of the earth and the sky, not marshmallows and despair." The newest arrival is below. In the meantime, if you like what you read here on oz.com, contribute to our operating costs. And thank you. -D.O.

OPENING DAY

Beaner strikes Pelota

with a big wooden gavel

bigger than his head

So it appeared

in color   above the fold

Yep!   the girl's vice principal is dead

the boy's v.p. is tougher

tougher on everything

it's the military-ecclesiastical complex

Jack Webb in "The D. I."   boy!

I wanted to kill him   how

could he talk to human beings like that?

Happens all the time

in the military-ecclesiastical complex

Everybody's an Authority Figure

back   down   over   there in DC

a Critical Mass

of Authority

a

military-ecclesiastical Mass

1/5/11

NONE OF THE ABOVE

Bergman's Blog, January 22, 2011

What if someone threw an election and nobody came? That's the way things are shaping up for the presidential election of 2012. By this time in 2006, nine candidates had already signed up for the race. Today, no one has thrown a hat or bonnet into the ring. How come?

For the last year and a half, Barack Obama has been taking nothing but grief from both sides of the political aisle, culminating in the November bloodbath that drove his party to the back benches in the House and reduced them to a precarious majority in the Senate. Mitch McConnell and John Boehner made it clear at the beginning of the 111th Congress that their mission was to mark Obama as a one-term president. So why aren't the GOP frontrunners putting on the cross and leading the crusade? Let's take a look.

MITT ROMNEY

Since his failed attempt to the lead the party in 2008, Mitt has been developing tremendous lower-body strength backpedaling from all the positions that made him a reasonably successful governor of Massachusetts. Obamacare is a first cousin of the plan Mitt put together for his home state, and the Tea Party is never going to let him forget it. Mitt's going to run, no doubt about it, but he can't be happy with his latest polling numbers. A couple of months ago he was neck-and-neck with Obama, and now he has fallen six points behind. Anyway, with all the self-consciously professing Christians in the pack, it'll be nice to have a Mormon besides Glenn Beck to kick around.

MIKE HUCKABEE

Mike turned his 2008 run for White House into a mega-career. When he won the Iowa caucus, he catapulted himself from the ranks of hick governor who dabbles in rock 'n' roll into the stratosphere of Fox talking-head, bestselling author and high paid motivational speaker, spreading his homely brand of genial, right-wing rhetoric. But Huck has a problem. In his own words, "I'm not going to run if I don't think I'm going to win." And the latest polls don't spell "winner." Like Romney, he's slipped from running head-to-head with the prez to the place horse five lengths behind. I hope he does run. He's the only bozo in that gaggle of boobs with a genuine sense of humor.

SARAH PALIN

Mama Grizzly, like The Huck, has done well for herself after John McCain did the country the unforgivable favor of elevating her to the VP slot. She is the darling of that 20 percent to 30 percent of the American public who would rather vote for Homecoming Queen or Perky Princess than president. They don't care that she quit being governor of Alaska on a whim, or that she's reckless, snide and paranoid-lite. That's what her followers like about her. The problem for Sarah is that a growing segment of the electorate doesn't like her and is losing trust in her as a potential leader. Sarah may be ignorant, but she's not dumb. She won't run, because she'll have to forgo making all that money, and in her heart, she knows that if she does grab the nomination she'll be crushed at the polls. That's bad for business, and The Winkie-Doll is all about business.

NEWT GINGRICH

The fact that The Newt is in contention for the nomination is proof positive of the ruinous state of affairs to which the Republican Party has sunk. Newt is a loose cannon from whose muzzle explodes a grapeshot of useful insights and megalomaniacal balderdash -- considerably more of the latter than the former. He crippled the GOP as House majority leader in the Clinton years and would lead them to ruin as a candidate in 2012. But, hey, if The Newt wants to diddle himself in the limelight and the GOP wants to court disaster, who am I to stand in the way?

TIM PAWLENTY

Polls show that people know little about T Paw because there's really not that much to know. He was re-elected governor of Minnesota in 2006 with 46 percent of the vote and has a book entitled "Courage To Stand" (does he have trouble standing?) that reached number 1976 on the Amazon bestseller list. Nuff said. Tim wants to cut Social Security and Medicaid, reinstate DADT, opposes gay marriage and thinks the Supreme Court got Roe vs. Wade all wrong. In other words, he is totally unelectable, which positions him as a frontrunner with all the other unelectables.

HALEY BARBOUR

What this pompous, antediluvian windbag does best is raise moolah for the party. He's the GOP's No. 1 money magnet and deserves all the perks the Republicans want to lay on him for sucking out the big bucks. But to encourage Haley to run for president is to court disaster. Do the Republicans really want him up there in the candidate debates waxing sentimental about the pre-civil-rights South and dismissing the oil sludge in the Gulf as "mousse?"

MIKE PENCE

Then there's this Indiana representative who describes himself as "a Christian, a conservative and a Republican, in that order." He is the Tea Party's wet dream: a total white man who could double for Richard the Lionhearted in a Robin Hood sequel, a foreign policy super-hawk, a hard-liner on immigration, an opponent of stem cell research and the favorite son of the arch-conservative Value Voters Forum. He doesn't have a snowball's chance in hell of of cadging a single Hispanic or African American vote, and he won't go down well with moderate independents, soccer moms, or anybody to the left of the militias and the birthers. But he looks good, speaks well -- he was a talk-show host in a former life -- and isn't burdened with a taste for irony or sense of humor. He could be the man to go up against the great Not-Me in the White House.

We'll have to wait and see.

GET THIS ONE PARTY STARTED

Bergman's Blog, March 17, 2011

Don't be fooled by the drubbing the GOP gave the Democrats in November. It was just a hiccup. We are watching the Republican Party melting down in front of our eyes.

Even if they weren't led by a bunch of bobble heads, bigots and corporate stooges whose antics are turning off every fair-minded citizen, the Republicans would still be doomed by the demographics. Their core constituency of over-fifty white dudes and dudettes is marching inexorably toward that happy home from which no voter returns.

They are being replaced by a rapidly growing cohort of wired X'ers, networked Millennials and no-nonsense, first-generation Americans who think that Rush and Glenn are odious gnomes, that God loves lesbians and gays, that a woman's right to choose is a given, that affordable health care is not a plot by Big Brother and that digging us out of this double-dip, deep-dish recession takes precedence over the right to bear extended clip assault rifles or the need to sniff out the President's birth certificate.

The turning point in the Republican's rush to destruction came in the mid-nineties when they rallied around Prop 186, California Governor Pete Wilson's attempt to criminalize the state's undocumented workers, bar them from emergency rooms and toss their children out of school. Their support of this cruel measure marginalized the GOP in California, and emboldened Republicans across the nation to come out of The Big Tent and declare their narrow minded nativism. Their ruthless xenophobia alienated the very Hispanic voters whose "family values" made them a logical target for GOP recruitment.

Then came Bush The Younger. Eight years of dry drunk stupidity, an illegal war, a drowned city, and a trashed economy. The election of Barack the Democrat was as much a signal of the center's disgust with Bush and his inner circle of seditious power brokers as it was their enthusiasm for the Messenger of Hope and Change.

And then the coup de grace, the rise of The Tea Party. Raging at the disappearance of white exceptionalism and unlimited credit, this gaggle of George Washington impersonators and gun show habitués drank the Koch Kool Aid and turned the midterm election on it's head. Result: five dozen, totally clueless, freshman Representatives and a handful of fresh wing-nuts in the Senate.

They soon revealed that it's one thing to win an election and another to govern. Less than three months in office and these fools are obviously over their heads, more passionate about trashing NPR and Planned Parenthood than creating jobs or educating the next generation.They're already eating their young, a beggar's banquet that will feed on itself for the next two years.

Come 2014, an underemployed, cash strapped and legitimately angry electorate will throw these bums out, return the Speakership to the dreaded Nancy Pelosi, increase the

Democrats grip on the Senate and return the great Not Me to the White House.

Then the dynamics within the Republican Party will reach critical mass and shatter. The Tea Party and the Ayatollahs will go their own way (perhaps to form a third party or parties) and what's left of the GOP will face a long sojourn in the wilderness.

It will be a one party Congress for a long, long time. Instead of donkeys and elephants it will be Green Democrats on the left, Blue Democrats in the center and Red Democrats on the right. Perhaps, in the short run, it could be a good thing. Certainly, Obama will need a strong mandate to turn this mess around. But after that, whither the two-party system? Your guess is as good as or better than mine.

THE VIEW FROM OIL PEAK MOUNTAIN
Bergman's Blog, March 24, 2011

We're bombing Libya, the Japanese are testing their spinach for radioactive iodine, gasoline is inching towards $5.00 a gallon, the housing market is at a nine year low, Charley Sheen is taking his Tiger Blood and Adonis DNA on the road, 30% of the smog on the West Coast is produced in China, the 400 wealthiest American households hold more assets than the bottom 60%, stocks of rice, the staple for half the world's population are at their lowest since the mid-70's and only 29% of the 1000 U.S. Citizens asked to take America's citizenship test could name the Vice President.(Joe, they hardly know ya)

In the midst of this world of woes, America is at its tipping point, tottering on the top of Mt. Peak Oil, poised to slide down its slippery slope into The Great Change, a world that few of us have envisioned and for which few of us are prepared.

What I have labeled The Great Change, the The Hopi Indians have long called The Purification. Forty years ago, a Hopi elder told me that when The Purification suddenly arrives, half of America will die on their hands and knees of a broken heart. I know that re-telling dismal Indian proficies qualifies me as a member of the Doom And Gloom Club. To quote John Boehner, "So be it." There are plenty of Panglossian pundits and think tank sychophants on tap to see light at the end of every free trade tunnel and crowds of neoliberal daffodils on every denuded hill.

These happy hacks are joined by the "Science Will Save Us" claque who claim we can solve all our problems by throwing sufficient numbers of white coats and money at 'em; "The Deniers" who believe all this fuss about global warming, shrinking resources, the growing divide between the Haves and the Have-Nothings and the breakdown of world order is so much liberal clap trap, and "The Second Comers" who merrily rape the earth, counting on the Jesus they've ginned up in their narrow, self-serving minds to return in the nick of time to instantly re-green the planet.

21st Century Americans are the product of a sixty year long shopping binge, underwritten by foreigners buying two billion dollars of T-Bills daily, and culturally supported by commercial television, the missionary of hyper-materialism. Under-informed and over-indulged, we join the Parade Of Fools, showing off the latest model of this or that, until we consign it to the landfill when it falls from fashion and favor. We are undoubtedly the least prepared for the social and economic upheavals that The Great Change will usher in.

But there is hope. Like Winston Churchill said, "You can count on Americans to do the right thing, after they've tried everything else." Well, buddy, we have tried everything else, and now it's a matter of survival that we do the right thing. Like, get more out of less, practice "small is beautiful," max out our library cards, cook a meal, feed the poor, pray for peace and put Big Brother on a diet by finding the lo-cal in local.

Open up my kimono of doom and gloom and you'll find an Ohio raised, corn fed,

American optimist. I believe in this land of plenty, as long as there's plenty for everyone. I believe in this government "of the people," as long as it's not "on the people." I believe in a free media and grass roots democracy as the antidote to mediocrity. I believe we can find the will and the spirit to confrontThe Great Change and come out on the other side a nation changed for the better. With these rose colored glasses on, I can see for miles and miles and miles.

MY WAY AND NO HIGHWAYS

Bergman's Blog, April 7, 2011

I'm writing this on the day before the government may or may not shut down. The whole enchilada is coming to a grinding halt because a gaggle of freshman Republicans won't compromise. "My golly," they say,"I can't go back to the folks in my district and tell them that since I've arrived here I've discovered that you've got to meet the other guy half way to get things done; not after I told them the other guy was working for the Devil."

The government closed down in 1995 because Newt Gingrich was a power hungry crazoid. Now, if the government collapses it will be because the Koch Brothers' cohort of billionaires, so ably led by their chief incubus, Karl Rove, and so conveniently enabled by a less that reputable majority on the Supreme Court have been able to whip up the boobs in the Tea Party into a white heat of anti-government invective. No surprise, the government is one of the few remaining tools whereby the shrinking middle class and the working poor can get some sort of social and economic justice. Cripple the government, break the unions-Classic Koch.

It's no coincidence that Paul Ryan nailed his draconian budget on the doors of Congress just as his colleagues were poised to throw their shows into The Machine. It's not the economy, stupid; it's something bigger. Let me limerize.

> Paul Ryan is giving us pause.
> His budget is loaded with flaws.
> But Ryan won't fudge it.
> Cause it's not a budget.
> To him it's a glorious cause.

Ryan proposes to decimate Medicare, murder Medacaid, and slash every sector of discretionary spending, while reducing the rates on the grossly under taxed super-rich. He's not insane, nor are the Tea Party Hearties; they're on a mission to save this country from itself.

And by the way, check out the fine print on the one-week, 30 billion dollar budget cutting continuing resolution they're trying to stuff down our throats; no condoms, no Big Brother clean air and no NPR, who just might report on what a bunch of witless yahoos they are. And put away those ready shovels, because they're not throwing any crumbs at the crumbling infrastructure. It's my way and no highways.

THE BULLY PULPIT VS.
THE SCHOOLYARD BULLIES

Bergman's Blog, April 13, 2011

There's been a lot of whinging and whining from the left end of the Democratic party. "Obama gave away the store; he's not a strong leader; he should have stood up to the GOP; he's not the man I voted for," and on and on.

You think he enjoyed giving up $38 billion dollars worth of well thought out and well led social programs? You think he had a choice? The majority over in House of Representatives are smoking loco weed and cow towing to those empty headed, Tea Party loud mouths. He may be the Speaker Of The House, but The Tan Woodman is scared to death of the trailer court crowd in the tri-corner hats. Boehner's the one who's shown a lack of leadership. He's the one who's been rolled by the likes of Michelle Bachmann and Trump The Toupee.

Most of the pundits-on-demand and barons of the blogoisie totally underestimate Obama's strategic acumen, or they're simply too busy blowing hard to thoroughly analyze the arena in which the President is engaged. He could have let the Republicans close down the government and take the heat for it, but to what end? Throw 800,000 federal workers on the street, disrupt the economy and frighten half the seniors to death to make a point, and a minor point at that?

In the struggle between the Democrats and the renegade right wing, the recent skirmish over funding the government through next September was strictly minor league. The Big Show is coming up-raising the debt ceiling and cobbling together a budget for 2012. Obama is positioning himself for these battle because he knows they really matter. He's going to fight them on his own terms with his weapons of choice. He's going to frame the debt ceiling fight in simple terms; make the rich pay their fair share of taxes or turn our Treasury notes into worthless T-Party bills.

The Republicans didn't score any points outside their base with their "my way and no highways" approach to negotiating with the Democrats. Independents know schoolyard bullies when they see them. And they ain't seen nothin' yet. John Boehner has already warned us he's willing to let the ceiling collapse, unless we wantonly slash the budget and wave goodbye to any programs the GOP's Moral Police abhor.

The American public got a good look at the Republican brinkmanship that nearly brought the government to a halt. They aren't going to cut them any slack when the time comes to stare default in the eye. The GOP, flushed with false victory, have won the bracelet and lost the high ground. They are about to get a lesson in The Art Of War, Obama style.

PUNKING THE GOP
Bergman's Blog, April 14, 2011

The day before the President spoke to the nation from George Washington University, I predicted that the GOP was about to get a lesson in the Art Of War-Obama style. Sure enough, in forty minutes, the Prez set the stage and the rules for any further budget and entitlement reform; and Paul Ryan got a front row seat to the punking of his seriously flawed and heartless Path To Prosperity.

Tax the rich, boldly spake the President, and get off the backs of senior Americans and the unfortunate. He drew a line in the wet concrete (setting as we speak); Medicare will not be crippled and Medicade will not be abolished during his watch. In doing so, he wound up his watch to run another four years.

And the Republican response ?

"He's too partisan!" Like the Republicans have been anything but partisan for the last two years, declaring Obama's defeat in 2012 their top priority.

"He's poisoning the waters for any future deal!" Those waters were poisoned long ago by all the precious bodily fluids that the GOP dumped on Obama's agenda, refusing to meet him half way on anything that didn't reflect their misogynistic, Bible thumping, plutocratic game plan.

"He's running for office instead of running the country!" You bet he is. He's up early, giving the reasonable souls in the electorate a clear choice between an articulate, unflappable and evenhanded candidate and the collection of fools, freaks and desperate back peddlers playing capture the flag for the Republican nomination.

You only have to look at the faces of Boehner, Cantor, McConnell and Ryan to see how thoroughly spooked they are. They expected the President to offer them the well worn olive branch so that they could snatch it, break it and throw it back in his face. Instead, he put them on the wrong side of the American Dream, where they are doomed to remain until the voters throw the bums out.

Since the Midterm shellacking, the GOP have been the toast of the town; now they're simply toast.

THE ART OF WAR- OBAMA STYLE

Bergman's Blog, April 19, 2011

This is a piece I composed for Politico's Arena blogging forum. It is a response to the question: "Why are Obama's numbers so low, and will he benefit by going on the road?"

President Obama's numbers are as low as they are because, true to form, he has taken a patient and thoughtful approach to our looming financial crisis, rather than pointing fingers and blowing hard like his detractors on the right and the left.

None of them have truly taken his measure, including the nervous and fickle electorate. They still blame him for the collapse of American exceptionalism and the hard times that have come in it's wake.

He's taken the heat; but last week at George Washington University, Obama drew a line in the setting cement. Thus spake the President. I will not extend the Bush tax cuts, and I call on the rich to pay their fair share of the burden. I will not allow Medicare to be crippled and Medicaid dismantled on my watch. In so speaking, Obama just wound up his watch for another four years.

Yes, his numbers are low, but look at the twenty plus points he's picked up with independent voters. Rational people don't want a Trump comb-over, a ginned up Tpaw-ty or an empty suit from Massachusetts who's developed immense lower body strength backpedaling from the little good he's done.

The Campaigner In Chief is going on the road, and his detractors are about to experience the Art Of War, Obama style.

A STAND-UP GUY WHO DOESN'T STAND A CHANCE

Bergman's Blog, April 20, 2011

Mitch Daniel's potential strengths in the upcoming Republican primaries are also his inherent weaknesses. In a contest that features The Donald, The Newt, The Sarah, The Mitt and The T-Paw, Mitch's record as a straight talking, generally moderate, reasonably intelligent and thoroughly experienced public servant puts him head and shoulders above the crowd of clowns, crazies and cowards playing Capture The Republican Flag.

Mitch harkens back to the days when the GOP put up sane and qualified leaders for the biggest job of all. He's one of those, and there's the rub. Having promoted higher taxes as part of a deficit reduction solution, having signed the Healthy Indiana Plan that bestowed health coverage on 132,000 working Hoosiers, and having called on the GOP for a truce on social issues (read,"Cool it on abortion, gay marriage and birther BS until we get our house in order"), Mitch has alienated himself from all the frustrated, know- nothing booboisie who will fill the Iowa caucuses and storm the New Hampshire polling booths.

Personally, I think Governor Daniels matches up pretty well with the current front runners. Unlike Trump, Mitch's hair and ideas are real; unlike Gingrich, Mitch doesn't struggle with the delusion that Obama is a crypto, Kenyan anti-colonialist; unlike Palin, Mitch can read; unlike Romney, Mitch has a spine and unlike Pawlenty, Mitch hasn't had his lips surgically attached to the posterior of the Mad Hatted Tea Party.

All in all, Mitch Daniels is a stand up guy who doesn't stand a chance.

NO, WE CANTOR

Bergman's Blog, April 21, 2011

Eric Cantor's prepared to play chicken with the nation's debt ceiling. Does this poor wonk fancy himself the newly risen James Dean, starring as the Beltway heart throb in "Rebel With A Cause?"

A cause that is nothing less than bringing down the Obama administration, the GOP's mission statement since 2008.

For two years in the minority the Republicans learned to "Just Say No." Now, in partial ascendancy, they're employing whatever means necessary to deny the Not Me in the White House a second term. It's not like the U.S. can't make good on their debts if we jack up the ceiling. With interest rates in the basement, this is a borrower's market; and with the Euro poised to slide on Greece and Japan's economy going nuclear, American T Bills remain the international hedge of choice.

Cluttering up the debt limit bill with more droppings from the defect hawks will only gum up the feeble recovery, and encourage Standard & Poors to downgrade our bonds below AAA? Wait a minute, isn't S&P the same gang of compliant toadies that slapped a Triple A rating on some of Wall Street's most toxic derivatives? Come on guys, give us a break. After all, what's good for the Golden Goose should be good for the Geitner.

I wonder who supports the Republican's commitment to financial brinkmanship. Maybe, it's the 20% of the country who have rallied behind the GOP's recent War On Medicare. So, ask your-self, "Can we afford to play chicken with these blinkered bullies and risk our economy taking a double dip in the deep fryer?" The answer is obvious. No, we Cantor.

SEND IN THE DRONES
Bergman's Blog, April 22, 2011

Send in the drones? Time magazine reports today that "the U.S. fired a volley of missiles into a militant-held region in Pakistan...ten missiles hit a house in Spinwam village...three children and two women were believed to be among the dead." Can we look forward to similar reports of collateral damage, replacing "Pakistan" with "Libya" and "Spinwam" with any one of the towns under siege from government forces?

This isn't mission creep, this is handing over the mission to the creeps who sit in refrigerated bunkers deciding who lives and who gets a Hellfire missile up their Kadafi-loving behind. And how can the joystick warriors tell the good guys from the bad guys? At twenty-five thousand feet it's hard to separate the black hats from the white.

As to whether the Libyan rebels have proven themselves worthy of our continuing support; that wasn't a consideration when we intervened in Bosnia or covertly supported the mixed bag of warlords and holy warriors in Afghanistan. Sure, the Libyan rebels are worthy; but are the protestors under the gun in Syria, Bahrain and Yemen any less worthy?

Yesterday, Mitt Romney empty suited-up, and accused Obama of "mission muddle" in Libya. It's a muddle all right, but not of our making. If Mitt and John Bolton and all the other soundbite strategists have a better plan, let's hear it. The silence is deafening.

ANOTHER BOZO EXITS THE GOP CLOWN CAR

Bergman's Blog, April 25, 2011

If Haley Barbour runs against Obama in 2012, it will be more of a trip, stumble and fall than a run.

Let us not forget, Barbour is the man who gazed out over the oil scum from the BP disaster and flippantly compared it to mousse. Barbour is the man who harkens back sentimentally to the days when the White Citizens Council kept things nice and normal in his Mississippi home town. Barbour is the Governor who has done little or nothing to improve his state's bottom of the barrel performance in education, health care and joblessness.

Yes, Haley's awfully good at collecting money for his fellow Republicans; but twisting arms and making secret deals with fat cats aren't skills that play well in Iowa and New Hampshire. When the campaign is over, Barbour will be remembered as just another political heavyweight who couldn't get his campaign off the ground.

LATE BREAKING NEWS!

ANOTHER BOZO EXITS THE GOP CLOWN CAR

Haley Barbour has taken a bow and gracefully exited the pack of Republican hopefuls, claiming that he has insufficient fire in his belly. Lots of belly, not enough fire.

Haley's no fool. He read the Tea Party leaves and found no auger of good fortune, even in the dregs, which is where his poll numbers reside. Now, he can go back to what he's really good at-being the GOP's number one financial flypaper. Roll him out at a Beltway bash, a Hilton Head hideaway or a corporate retreat and Barbour comes back loaded with billionaire bucks and corporate cash, which he dutifully dispenses to his colleagues who have stayed on the stump, taking his vig out in favors down the line.

I suspect that more than one Republican ringleader is not unhappy to see Haley exiting the Big Tent. They must have an inkling of what a haircut the party would take if Barbour made the cut.

EVERY DARK HORSE HAS ITS DAY
Bergman's Blog, April 26, 2011

Isn't Ron Paul a stitch? I'm so glad he's entering the race for the GOP nomination. He'll bring a refreshing candor to the process. As a progressive and civil libertarian there are many issues on which I think Rep. Paul is spot on-legalization of recreational drugs, a radical curtailing and restructuring of the out of control intelligence community, a retreat from nation building abroad, a thorough pruning of the bloated defense budget and an end to bailing out the toxic con men on Wall St.

On others issues, most of which concern entitlements, federal funding for education, research, workplace safety and the like, Ron and I are one-eighty. Some of his ideas I find so out of touch with reality that I wonder what he's smoking; but Ron and I agree that's none of my business.

Welcome on board, Congressman. The pundits say you don't stand a chance, maybe not; but you'll keep the rest of the field honest, and, who knows-every Dark Horse has it's day.

DOES THE OVAL OFFICE FACE MECCA?
Bergman's Blog, April 28, 2011

We'll have to wait and see if the President put the birther issue to rest by trotting out his birth certificate. I suspect The Donald will soon be calling for Obama's report cards from the Kenyan or Indonesian madrassa where a whole chunk of Americans are convinced he was schooled.

A plurality of Republicans actually believe that Barack Hussein Obama is a crypto-Muslim. Even if we followed the President every Sunday with a church-cam, the word would get out that he had repositioned his desk in the Oval Office to face Mecca. In August of last year, Mitch McConnell did no better than declare, "If the President says he's a Christian, I'll take him at his word." Fine, if Mitch contends he's anything but a spineless, partisan hack, I'll cut him the same slack.

It's hard to judge whether the Democrats did their part in denouncing the ridiculous claims that Bush knew 9/11 was coming. Those rumors didn't crowd the front page or top anybody's news hour; they remained deep in the sordid world of fusion paranoia, where the lunatic fringes of the left and the right meet.

As long as our culture honors the dumb and dumber, as long as the principles of fair and balanced remain a cynical marketing ploy, the dogs of rumor and innuendo will have their day.

YOU'LL HAVE TO TALK TO MY BODY

Bergman's Blog, Previously Unpublished

In the late 60's, The Firesign Theatre released an album entitled, Waiting For The Electrician Or Someone Like Him. The title came from a script of mine in which some unexpected, inevitable force comes along and pulls the big electrical plug. Just a couple of days ago, it happened to me. The corner power station caught on fire, and that pulled the plug on my life for a day.

Everything shut down at once-the lights, the television, the heating system, the kitchen appliances (the stove is gas but functions electrically), the hot water, and the garage door opener. The power went out in the morning, so my inner clock immediately began countig down the hours before the darkening of the light.

I felt truly helpless. My "living better through electricity" life had stopped, and there was nothing I could do about it. My thoroughly modern brain told me that this glitch in the grid was no more than a temporary pain in the ass; but my cave man body was sending an entirely different set of signals. My body goes way back. It is totally Old School, and has never been happy living in a city that counts on everybody else and everywhere else to feed its belly, slake its thirst, fill its tanks, stock its stores and deliver gigawatts of electricity to power its fabulously unsustainable life style.

My body figured out long ago that my urban setting, pleasant as it was couldn't keep me alive on it's own. My body was right! The power's out. What can I do to survive? Cut down the trees that line street for firewood? They're too green to burn, and my fireplace is only fit for dummy logs. Hunt the neighbors pets and the opossums in the philodendron for meat? In these End Times, I'll need all the local good will I can gather, and I don't have a receipt for opossum. Switch to candles and kerosene lamps? The only candles in the house are what's left of my ex-girlfriend's aroma-theraputc votaries. Lincoln would have gone blind trying study law by them.

A bonfire at my corner power station in no way compares to six nuclear reactors shattered and drowned by the one-two punch of a 9.1 earthquake and a 30 foot, 500 mph tsunami. But tell that to my body. My brian may be satisfied whipping up logical, theoretical or fanciful explanations of the situation; but my body wants to know where's the food, the drink and the dry, warm shelter.

I've just returned to Los Angeles after living for a year and a half on an island off Seattle at the north end of the Puget Sound. No buildings over two stories, the maximum height from which my body can jump without necessarily killing itself; no multi-lane freeways filled with people driving too fast or two slow or on the phone or on drugs or on their way to sleep; and no lack of locally grown food, clean water, friendly businesses and able, helpful neighbors. Living there was a psychic vacation for my prehistoric, city-stressed body.

For all of that, I'm back in L.A. I love this town; but every time I ride up to the 50th floor of some glass clad skyscraper to take a meeting, or run out to the local supermarket to buy the staples that my ancestors grew, raised, baked and cured for countless generations; or shed my shoes, my belt and every piece of metal I carry on my body that I might pass through a hail of X-rays to board an aluminum tube and hurtle thirty- five thousand feet above the ground that my feet know so well, my born at the dawn of time body reminds me what a fragile existence I'm living.

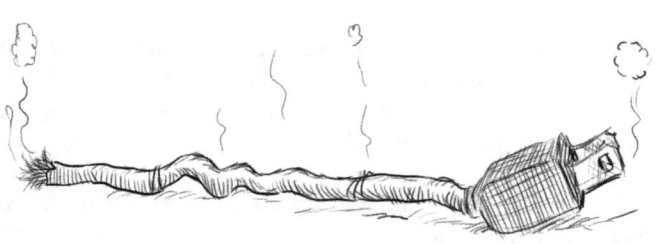

NO OLD FOLKS IN PARADISE
By David Ossman

Hello, Dear Friends. This is Rev. Bill Barnstormer of the First 2nd Amendment Church of Science – Fiction.

Well, Dear Friends, not so long ago a believer came to me – say thank you for that – and asked me, "What age will I be in Heaven?" and I pondered that question and considered how the Five Justices of the Apocalypse might decide – and it came down to me from that great Court that there will be NO old folks in Heaven – no, sir, and say thank you for that!

And I told my parish'ner, when you meet your forebears, friends and relations in that Fully-Loaded Paradise to come, know that it's in the Constitution – life, liberty and the pursuit of happiness – and that's only a sure thing if you look your best. "So as ye see yourself, so shall ye be!"

So when you get there, don't ask the ladies about nippin' and tuckin', or why all the men got the pecs they always wanted. It's their right as Americans in Paradise and say thank you for that!

This is Rev. Bill Barnstormer, sayin', send for my free "I'm afraid of" bumper stickers in three choices – "illegal aliens," "real aliens," and "arms control." Send for one today to PO Box 5 against 4, Arroyo Mio, Arizona. Your donation helps the fight.

THE NEW NEW DEAL- EDUCATION POLICY 2.0
Bergman's Blog, Previously Unpublished

There 's a man I know who runs a high tech chip and circuit company in Boston. He sits on the panel at a prestigious university, judging the oral dissertations of graduate students in the field of thin film physics-a key discipline in the global marketplace. Here's the zinger. Over the last decade, not one graduate student who's appeared before his panel was born and raised in America. Lots from China, Egypt, Palestine and India, not one from America.

No surprise. For the last fifty years we have stopped learning how to design and build real goods and concentrated on marketing and consuming other people's inventions and products. Nobody on television-our modern role models-actually makes anything, except for the occasional bozo pimping up a thoroughly serviceable 4-door into a candy apple Batmobile.

The G.I. drafted into World War II had a higher average IQ than any of his counterparts dragooned into Korea, Vietnam, Iraq and Afghanistan. We're dumbing down, and the dumber we get the less we seem to notice or care. And who benefits? The same fat cats and political overlords who are grinding the middle class into poverty and incarcerating vast minions of the underclass-that's who.

The poor, the uneducated and the incarcerated rarely vote, and certainly aren't organizing to seriously reform the system that has them so thoroughly in thrall. Throughout history, it's the educated middle class that has supplied us with our most potent reformers.

We have to stand up to all this this dumbing down. Here's my solution. Please keep in mind that all the programs below will be paid for in great part by the increased tax revenue generated by the New New Deal tax policies. (See previous blog The New New Deal-Tax Policy on radiofreeoz.com)

The New New Deal-Education Policy

GUARANTEE COLLEGE AND GRADUATE SCHOOL EDUCATIONS TO ALL QUALIFIED CANDIDATES

Offer low interest students loans to all students who qualify for college and/or graduate school. Then offer the opportunity for the graduates to pay off their loans with stints of national service in their various disciplines. We pay your way through medical school, you pay off the loan bringing medical services to the sick and needy. It' a win-win. The same format works for any discipline. Young teachers, engineers, writers, lawyers and MBA's, to name only a few, spreading out across the country, contributing their newly acquired skills to the Commonwealth that has put them through school.

REQUIRE THAT ALL HIGH SCHOOL AND COLLEGE GRADUATES MASTER A PRACTICAL, TECHNICAL SKILL

I hated woodworking and metal shop in high school because everyone knew it had nothing to do with what we were going to do with our lives. What would a middle class snob like myself, headed for the Ivy League, give a damn about making a solid weld? Times have changed, buddy. If we want to take back this country and heal it, we better get some of those healing skills under our belts. It may not be auto shop-unless you're intent on pimping your Prius-but how about horticulture, basic carpentry, cooking, sustainable landscaping-the list goes on and on. The point is that we either are taught to grow, make and repair some of our own, or we'll end up a nation of useless dandies, flipping burgers, flipping fingers and flipping out.

A STROLL DOWN THE PATH TO PROSPERITY
Bergman's Blog, April29, 2011

There's no doubt that the shellacking the Republicans are taking at town hall meetings is the real thing. You tell seniors and the generations behind them that you're going to cripple Medicare and murder Medicaid so you can give a trillion dollar tax break to the rich, and you won't have to hire any agent provocateurs to get the party started.

In 2009, the GOP had to terrorize the public with the specter of Death Panels playing Beat The Reaper with the elderly to whip up any substantial opposition to Obamacare. Now, the Dems only have to read directly from Paul Ryan's delusional and statistically flawed plan for the future to fan the flames of discontent.

What was John Boehner thinking when he allowed his party to vote in lock step for this toxic bill? I actually thought the Tan Woodman had more political savvy than that. And now, Harry Reid, the wily fox, is going to make his Republican colleagues choose whether or not to take a stroll down "The Path To Prosperity," a journey not unlike walking the plank into a sea of angry voters waiting to eat you alive. Bon appetite. hated woodworking and metal shop in high school because everyone knew it had nothing to do with what we were going to do with our lives. What would a middle class snob like myself, headed for the Ivy League, give a damn about making a solid weld? Times have changed, buddy. If we want to take back this country and heal it, we better get some of those healing skills under our belts. It may not be auto shop-unless you're intent on pimping your Prius-but how about horticulture, basic carpentry, cooking, sustainable landscaping-the list goes on and on. The point is that we either are taught to grow, make and repair some of our own, or we'll end up a nation of useless dandies, flipping burgers, flipping fingers and flipping out.

THE NEW NEW DEAL- EDUCATION POLICY 2.0

Bergman's Blog, Previously Unpublished

There 's a man I know who runs a high tech chip and circuit company in Boston. He sits on the panel at a prestigious university, judging the oral dissertations of graduate students in the field of thin film physics-a key discipline in the global marketplace. Here's the zinger. Over the last decade, not one graduate student who's appeared before his panel was born and raised in America. Lots from China, Egypt, Palestine and India, not one from America.

No surprise. For the last fifty years we have stopped learning how to design and build real goods and concentrated on marketing and consuming other people's inventions and products. Nobody on television-our modern role models-actually makes anything, except for the occasional bozo pimping up a thoroughly serviceable 4-door into a candy apple Batmobile.

The G.I. drafted into World War II had a higher average IQ than any of his counterparts dragooned into Korea, Vietnam, Iraq and Afghanistan. We're dumbing down, and the dumber we get the less we seem to notice or care. And who benefits? The same fat cats and political overlords who are grinding the middle class into poverty and incarcerating vast minions of the underclass-that's who.

The poor, the uneducated and the incarcerated rarely vote, and certainly aren't organizing to seriously reform the system that has them so thoroughly in thrall. Throughout history, it's the educated middle class that has supplied us with our most potent reformers.

We have to stand up to all this this dumbing down. Here's my solution. Please keep in mind that all the programs below will be paid for in great part by the increased tax revenue generated by the New New Deal tax policies. (See previous blog The New New Deal-Tax Policy on radiofreeoz.com)

The New New Deal-Education Policy

GUARANTEE COLLEGE AND GRADUATE SCHOOL EDUCATIONS TO ALL QUALIFIED CANDIDATES

Offer low interest students loans to all students who qualify for college and/or graduate school. Then offer the opportunity for the graduates to pay off their loans with stints of national service in their various disciplines. We pay your way through medical school, you pay off the loan bringing medical services to the sick and needy. It' a win-win. The same format works for any discipline. Young teachers, engineers, writers, lawyers and MBA's, to name only a few, spreading out across the country, contributing their newly acquired skills to the Commonwealth that has put them through school.

OSAMA'S DEAD, MEDUSA'S NEXT

Bergman's Blog, May 2, 2011

If the primary goal of our anti-terrorism campaign is to crush Al Qaida, then keeping two billion dollars a week worth of boots on the ground in Afghanistan won't get that done. Propping up Karzai and taming the Taliban are off mission when it comes to neutralizing Al Qaida.

Increasing our military presence in Yemen is also counterproductive, because as Bin Laden made abundantly clear, the goal of Al Qaida is not "winning a war" with America, but regaining the Islamic Caliphate that once stretched from the Hindu Kush to the gates of Vienna. Al Qaida needs a worldwide uprising of the faithful to realize that dream, and goading the U.S. into increasing their unwelcome presence in Islam is a means to that end.

What we need to destroy Al Qaida worldwide is better coordination and analysis of the massive amounts of human and signal intelligence we collect every day. What good are the telephone calls that the NSA intercepts from Morocco to Islamabad, if they lack the Arabic, Urdu, and Pashtun speakers to translate them?

And once analyzed, what good is that info if it lies scattered among the multiple agencies that comprise our intelligence community? I'm glad Bin Laden is dead; but Al Qaida is not a snake that perishes when it's head is severed. With its network of poisonous cells, it's more like a Medusa, that can only be killed when all the snakes that spring from it's head are crushed.

THE LOW ROAD TO ABBOTTABAD
Bergman's Blog, May 3, 2011

I doubt we'll ever know if water boarding played a part in Bin Laden's assassination, unless the CIA and the DOD want to come clean on their use of the darker arts. If, as reported, the clues that led to the compound in Abbottabad came from Guantanamo interrogations, then the more calloused among us will grasp on our success as a rationale for continuing to torture America's prisoners. I grew up on WW II films in which only wicked Japanese officers and Gestapo sadists did such terrible things.

Haven't we learned anything from Abu Ghraib? The charming photos of Muslims being tortured and sexually assaulted sabotaged our efforts to stabilize Iraq. If it's revealed that we water boarded our way to Bin Laden, we will be giving substance to Al Qaida's caricature of us as ruthless, Christian crusaders. The low road may have taken us to Abbottabad, but I shudder to think where that perilous path will lead us in the future.

LET'S PLAY "HIDE THE TERRORIST"

Bergman's Blog, May 4, 2011

Pakistan has been playing us like a violin since we butted into the Afghan war to rub Russia's nose in their own private Vietnam. We didn't know the territory, didn't speak the languages and couldn't tell one warlord from another. We arrived loaded down with cash and pumped up with cowboy bravado- perfect marks for Pakistani Intelligence. We didn't realize that Pakistan's Afghan involvement was all about Kashmir. They needed our endless supply of bucks to have a say in post Russian Afghanistan and recruit volunteers among the mujahideen for their holy war with India.H

Jump ahead twenty years and the U.S. is back to take out the Taliban and the Al Qaida training camps. The CIA, having forgotten about Afghanistan in the interim had to send back the same old hands who ran the show in the 80's. These Cold Warriors quickly got back in bed with their old mentors, Pakistani Intelligence.

It's common knowledge that Pakistan has been double crossing us for years, supporting the very warlords who kill American soldiers, training the Taliban and hiding Al Qaida big wigs. It's a little late for finger wagging at Pakistan and threatening them with sanctions. It's strategically stupid to boot. We need them to control their border if we ever hope to contain the Taliban. We need them to keep their nukes at home, and we need them at the negotiating table with India if we ever hope to broker a lasting peace in Asia.

Now that we've caught them playing "Hide The Terrorist," maybe we can get Pakistan to hand over the other Al Qaida leaders vacationing in their country. Fondly to be hoped; but whatever they do, we're stuck with these buzzards, like it or not.

I SELL ENCYCLOPEDIAS, REALLY. ENCYCLOPEDIAS.

BIRDS, BEES AND THE STRAIGHT POOP FROM REV. BARNSTORMER

This is Rev. Bill Barnstormer of the First Non-Sexterian Church of Science – Fiction.

And speaking of Sex, who isn't? Say "Thank You" for that! Right now they're talking about Sex in State Capitols, Supreme Courts and even the Pentagon! Don't kid yourselves, Dear Friends, the whole Adam and Eve lesson is about not having Sex with each other, except to have children, and say "Thank You" for that – even if the kids do kill each other and can't seem to hold onto a steady job.

So, our Dear Friends and Neighbors who righteously believe that marrying is only and exclusively between a so-called Man and a self-professed Woman of opposite genders – well, Dear Friends, that's because the other kind doesn't make children, say "Thank You", and their unspeakable ways of copulating are no fit subject for Man or Beast – or worse!

So they's only one answer – those of us who oppose same-sex marriage are simply disgusted by the oratal-genital way of life, not to mention body parts I won't mention, and say "Thank You" for that!

Now down to the Pentagon, well, since our Army learned how to re-build whole societies, formerly known only to readers of the National Geographic, right from the village schoolhouse on up to military compounds bigger than an Arizona border settlement, it needs school marms and visiting nurses and nutritionists and wives!

It does not need good men having to look surreptitiously around the big, naked locker-room of naked men to see if other men are looking at them surreptitiously. It's bad for morale! And it shrinks the body parts! Say "Thank You" for that!

So, please, Dear Friends, if you profess to be gay – and some of my former close friends are – stay out of the U. S. Army. There's nothin' gay about war. Say "Thank You" for that!

Write soon for your free book to keep and protect with your unconcealed sidearm, "Restore A Compassion-Free America" as told to Ayn Rand and Rand Paul, send a postcard with the words "Drill 'em, Baby, Drill 'em," to Big, Tall, Immense Electrified Fence, Texas, Zip.

And while you're in the mood, send for my free "I'm afraid of" bumper stickers in three choices – "illegal aliens," "real aliens," and "arms control." Send for one today to PO Box 5 against 4, Arroyo Mio, Arizona. Your donation helps the fight.

BIRDS AND BEES...

THE ZERO WON'T COME TO GROUND
Bergman's Blog, May 5, 2011

Inviting George Bush to the Ground Zero ceremony is in line with President Obama's efforts to bring the country together. I won't speculate on the reasons for Bush's refusal; but he must be aware that many Republicans are trying to diminish Obama's success in bringing down Bin Laden by lathering their praise on George W. while ignoring the President's efforts entirely.

In the name of closing the yawning, partisan gap between the administration and the gaggle of mean spirited ignoramuses and self-inflating hucksters who remain the dominant mouthpiece of the GOP, I would advise President Bush to come to New York and stand beside the man who finished the job he began.

WEARING THE SCARLET "U"
Bergman's Blog, May 6, 2011

Nine percent is the "official" unemployment rate, concocted to put a brave and reality-free face on a rapidly developing crises among jobless Americans. Two facts to keep in mind; the number of those unemployed for over a year are at a record high and at the present rate of adding two hundred thousand plus jobs a month, we won't return to post recession levels of employment until sometime around 2020. That's a mighty long time for the unemployed to wait for their ship to come in.

Is the economy stagnant? Absolutely. Most of the newly added jobs are low-paid and low-skilled positions. Professionals are taking major salary cuts and significant demotions in the business food chain to get any work at all. And it's only going to get worse for the long-tern unemployed. A year out of the game, they lose their network of business contacts, lose touch with new or upgraded software and come to job interviews wearing a scarlet "U" on their breasts. More and more companies are looking for new hires among the already employed.

The Republican House is doing everything it can to exacerbate the problem. President Obama had to extend the morally repugnant Bush tax cuts to get a measly extension of unemployment benefits. The Ryan Express is all about coddling the rich and shredding the safety net; so until we oust the compassionless reactionaries from Congress, it's going to be no-business- as- usual for the long term unemployed. And in the long term, quoth Lord K, we are all dead.

THE DEVIL AND THE DETAILS
Bergman's Blog, May 9, 2011

If George Bush had successfully tracked Osama Bin Laden to his redoubt and taken him out, do you think the Democrats would have wasted their time complaining about the details that came out of the dust and blood of that desperate mission? And think of the thunder of chest thumping that would have rolled out of that White House of Washington warriors. The President would have had MISSION ACCOMPLISHED! tattooed on his brow to remind everyone that he got something right after all.

The Republicans are gobsmacked by the breadth of the administration's success. The classic picture of Obama and his advisors looking so very much on point as they follow the assassination at Abbottabad will haunt the GOP in 2012. How are they going to explain to their rabid base that the ineffective, collectivist sissy in the White House took down the terrorist whose face had graced every dartboard and shooting range target in America. Let me sum it up in rhyme.

> *America's gotten it's wish.*
> *Osama now sleeps with the fish.*
> *The Prez is a winner,*
> *When he sits down to dinner,*
> *There's no humble pie in his dish*

THE NOT-ME STANDS UP FOR "THE OTHERS"

Bergman's Blog, May 10, 2011

It's possible that the President's decision to go to Texas to promote immigration reform may be as political as it is passionate, but where's the surprise? One bully pulpit versus two-hundredplus bullies in the House is the reality that Obama has to work with. No meaningful immigration reform is going to happen until the Democrats control both houses of Congress, and that's only going to come about if the President keeps and increases his hold on the Hispanic vote.

You'd think the Republicans would read the demographic tea leaves and change their well earned image as nasty, Limbaugh-led xenophobes. The birther brouhaha that Boehner and McConnell winked at, and The Donald trumped, has so poisoned the GOP's relationship with America's immigrant community that the Elephant may never graze in that neighborhood again.

It's a good thing that the Democratic Hispanic caucus is keeping the heat on Obama. He has the power to stop the deportation of undocumented college students and young illegals who would qualify for citizenship once the Dream Act gets the nod. Who better than the "Not-Me" in the White House, whose citizenship and patriotism has been slandered and libeled by the wing-nuts on the Right, to defend our immigrant community, under attack from the same ill-informed and unforgiving souls.

INTO THE GREAT BLUE WONDER

Bergman's Blog, May 11, 2011

That President Obama would ruminate publicly about spending time and treasure in Texas highlights two political realities, one structural, one accidental.

Structurally, the entire chunk of the Southwest that the Lone Star rebels and the U.S. Army wrenched from Mexico has become an increasingly solid Hispanic enclave, worth a whopping 118 electoral votes. Add those to the 126 that the Northeast and Illinois consistently deliver, and the Democrats are a mere 28 votes away from grabbing the Big Enchilada.

The accidental factor that puts Texas in play is the total disarray of the Republican Party. Their leader in the House is bemoaning the lackluster quality of the gang singing up for the primaries. Their wagon is hitched to the unpredictable, uninformed and unrelenting

Tea Party, that requires total submission to its nativist dogma from any candidate who doesn't what to see their votes drained away by a well funded insurgent, campaigning on their right.

If the GOP pick a thoroughly unelectable candidate with the coattails of a Speedo, and run on a platform that only a dyed in the wool Social Darwinist could love, they will drive independents and moderate Republicans out of the Big Tent and into Obama's arms; and then, maybe, perhaps, the state that has seen red for twenty years will cross the purple divide into the great blue wonder.

DEAR MR. PRESIDENT
Bergman's Blog, May 12, 2011

Dear, Mr. President,

I've been a solid supporter of yours ever since you entered the fray in 2008; so, rest assured, that what follows comes from a friend.

You're an exceptionally smart person, well educated, well read and well informed. Although the presidency is by nature an ivory tower job, your time community organizing on the streets of Chicago schooled you in the everyday reality of less fortunate Americans.

I know you took office after eight years of corrupt government that lied to us, swindled us and sent our fellow Americans to die in a war based on falsehoods and treachery. I know the economy was in a shambles, thanks to the criminal conspiracy engineered by the mortgage and banking cabals. You know it too, and so does your former Secretary of the Treasury, Larry Summers, who was snout deep in the whole sordid affair.

I know your party took a drubbing in the midterms, fueled by the millions of anonymous dollars set free by a Supreme Court that harbors those suborned Koch dealers, Thomas and Scalia.

When the patrician, FDR fashioned the New Deal to fight poverty and injustice, he was branded a traitor to his class. You're a middle class kid, leading a nation where the middle class is under siege. We're being squeezed, cheated and ground down; and if you don't come to our aid, then you're at risk of betraying your own.

I know you had to extend the odious Bush tax cuts in order to eke a smidgeon more unemployment benefits out of that collection of heartless skinflints, who have wiggled their way into congress.

You have to do what you have to do; but, paste some on, Mr. President. If you don't stop the plutocrats and ideologues from transforming this once vibrant democracy into a fiefdom for the greedy, amoral one-percent who own ninety-five percent of our working assets, then you'll have reneged on your promise of "hope" and "change."

What are you afraid of-a one term presidency? You're selling Americans short if think they'll abandon you if you stand up to the Tan Woodman and his cronies in the House, who are threatening us with default if we don't dismantle fifty years worth of key social programs. Give those Ayatollahs Hell, Mr. President!

I sure would like to be a fly on the debt ceiling when you do.

MACWORLD TALE
Bergman's Blog, May 13, 2011

I just noticed that *Macworld* has joined the "Like" crew on the Radio Free Oz Facebook page. Let me tell you my *Macworld* tale.

I was made an Apple Master in 2001 and opened the *Macworld* convention in San Francisco. Just me and Steve Jobs on stage. I look out and there on the far wall is the giant Apple logo. Suddenly, it comes to me. I say, " Hey, I just figured out what that slice in the Apple represents...our market share." A shocked silence settled over the Mac nerds in the audience. Then, Steve Jobs started to laugh, and the whole place came apart.

LET SLIP THE DOGGERELS OF WOE

Bergman's Blog, May 13, 2011

Tom Coburn is quitting the Gang
Compromising is just not his thang.
  He refuses to play,
  If he can't get his way,
And resolving the mess can go hang.

The Prez of the IMF vault
Is in handcuffs for rape and assault.
  And Arnold's a Dad
  With the housemaid he had,
Does power breed sin by default?

Newt's throwing his hat in the ring.
What could prompt him to do such a thing?
  Imagine the stink
  When they open Newt Inc.
And the two wives he screwed start to sing.

Ron Paul wants to dump Medicare,
And legalize smack; now, that's fair.
  All the poor uninsured,
  Won't be treated or cured;
They'll just shoot up and not really care.

Paneta is DOD bound,
To keep budgets and boots on the ground.
  They've given Petraeus
  The CIA dais,
Just moving the old drones around.

MISSING MIKEY
Bergman's Blog, May 15, 2011

I'll miss the Huck. He's the only one of the GOP hopefuls with any Elvis in him. Mikey plays a decent rock and roll bass, and has a winning sense of humor. But, below his charming patina of folksy wit and good fellowship lies a dangerous, dyed in the wool theocrat.

Case in point. Huckabee once joked that he answers to "two Janets"- his wife, Janet Huckabee and Janet Porter, the onetime co-chair of his Faith and Values Coalition. Porter, whom Huckabee calls his "prophetic voice," warned that Democrats want to throw Christians in jail for practicing their faith, attributed Haiti's high poverty rate to their dedication to Satan, suggested that gay marriage caused Noah's Flood and revealed that Barack Obama is a Soviet secret agent, groomed since birth to destroy the United States from within. Nuf said?

Mike put Porter on a short list of evangelicals, including Tim LaHaye, who made his rise possible. Perhaps it was LaHaye who consoled Huckabee to sacrifice the rapture of running for the Fox bucks and lecture lucre waiting for him if he chose to join the Left Behind.

NEWT'S UNFRIENDLY FIRE
Bergman's Blog, May 17, 2011

Newt Gingrich has always been a loose canon. He's only newsworthy now because he's turned his weapon one-eighty, spraying the GOP with friendly fire. Where was the right wing umbrage when Gingrich accused the President of being a Kenyan trained anti-colonialist?

The Republicans are happy to let the Little Professor run at the mouth, as long as he keeps his invective focused on the Dems. But, when Newt calls out the radical social engineering underlying Paul Ryan's "Path to Plutocracy," every mouthpiece on the right cries foul.

It's fun to have the unpredictable windbag from Georgia on board. Newt's hyperactive, unregulated brain can be counted on to produce a slew of controversial ideas, and his unregulated mouth guarantees they'll be given voice.

Gingrich alone is brave (or reckless) enough to call out Ryan's Contract On Medicare and to support state mandated health insurance, a plan that Mitt Romney brought to Massachusetts, and from which he has been backpedaling ever since. All in all, faced with the sleep inducing collection of Republican candidates, it's a real boon to have Newt around to rouse the rabble.

MAD HATTERS AT THE T-PAWTY
Bergman's Blog, May 23, 2011

The joker in this equation is the Tea Party. They're really good at punishing politicians who veer an iota from their narrow orthodoxy. They took out Bennett in Utah in the Midterms, and will probably hand a safe Republican seat to the Democrats tomorrow.n

I didn't take them seriously when they emerged two years ago. They appeared a quirky gathering of angry, over fifty-five whites, frustrated with the collapse of the bubble economy; convinced that all their problems could be traced back to the Not Me in the White House.

I was wrong. The Tea Party and their right wing agenda aren't going away. How does this auger for Pawlenty, Romney and Huntsman, the three establishment candidates? The kooks in the tri-corner hats wrote Mitt off long ago, and Huntsman may be fatally flawed because he heeded the call of our crypto Muslim President to placate the communists in far off Cathay.

That leaves T-Paw, who's done his damnedest to kiss the Tea Party's ring. He's performed his mea culpas for protecting the environment, and is parroting the cant of draconian budget cuts and tax relief for the rich. But it won't be enough. Pawlenty, bless his beige, Minnesota persona, isn't crazy enough for the Tea Party. If they can't convince Bachmann or Palin to lead a third party, they'll write them in, or do whatever they can to spoil the GOP's chances in 2012, and perhaps for decades thereafter.

A TRAP MORE THAN A PATH
Bergman's Blog, May 26, 2011

If the special election in New York's 26th is to be taken seriously, then the Republican Senators who signed on to Paul Ryan's radical restructuring of Medicare are in for a rough time. Why else would Harry Reid have forced a vote of a bill that was dead on arrival in the Senate, except to put the opposition on record supporting a plan rejected by seventy percent of Americans. It could bring Dick Lugar down. This decent man is already a target of the Tea Party and now has put himself on the wrong side of the majority of Hoosier seniors and independents.

The Democrats aren't going to let this issue go. In the debacle in upstate New York, the GOP outspent them two to one and lost by four points in a district that Chris Lee dominated in the midterms. A lot can happen in the next seventeen months; but every day that the election draws near is another day that the under fifty-five electorate grows older and closer to the time when Medicare will be a matter of life and death. The "Path To Prosperity" may be the road to nowhere for the Republicans in 2012.

A DARK HORSE OF ANOTHER COLOR

Bergman's Blog, May 27, 2011

I vividly recall the two times I feared for the future of this country. The first, the nightmare of the Cuban missile crisis; and the second, the vice presidential candidacy of Sarah Palin, potentially placing her a mere seventy-year old, myocardial heartbeat away from the Big Button. Fortunately, Khrushchev blinked, and the American electorate denied Sarah the White House.

Palin is making noises about running again, but I don't believe she's serious. Running for the presidency is not her strong suit. She'd have to read all those nasty position papers, take a humongous pay cut and couldn't go clothes and jewelry shopping on her campaign credit card, without the whole world watching. I predict that Sarah will take a pass.

Michelle Bachmann is a dark horse of another color. She's the queen of the tea party, a spirited speaker, formidable fund raiser, faithful spouse, and sharp tongued warrior, ever ready to do battle with our "Un-American" President.

She's going to be a whole lot of fun to have around in the campaign season. Once Newt implodes completely and Cain fails to deliver, it will be up to Michelle to take up the radical right wing slack and keep the carnival going.

A DEBT THAT'S OVERDUE

Bergman's Blog, May 31, 2011

One good stunt deserves another. Senators Boxer and Casey know they're constitutionally restricted from pink slipping their esteemed colleagues until the debt ceiling is lifted. Similarly, Republicans, with only a scintilla of economic sense, realize that failing to raise the debt ceiling could trigger a worldwide flight from T-Bills and the dollar.

But, after holding the budget hostage until they'd exacted their revenge on the infrastructure and us sub-millionaires, the GOP's fiscal ayatollahs are back at the brink, threatening to lower our government's credit rating unless we savage Medicare and other programs that serve the shrinking middle class and embattled, working poor.

The only sure and constitutionally approved means of denying ample paychecks and gilt edged health plans to Boehner, McConnell, Cantor, Ryan and their compassion free brethren is to vote them out of office as soon as possible. It's a debt we owe our country and our future.

A SEVENTH DWARF STAR?
Bergman's Blog, June 1, 2011

It's a sad commentary on the state of the present day GOP that any buzz at all should be raised by the rumor that Texas Governor Rick Perry might throw his ten gallon into the ring. The man is a total non-starter; just ask 96% of the Lone Star Republicans, recently polled on the issue. They don't want him to run, and they're the voters who know him best.

If Rick is the Snow White that the GOP are desperately seeking, then he put his White House dreams to sleep forever when he bit down on the poisoned secessionist apple. I can't imagine that anyone, save the party's hard core loonies, would support a man who honors the sesquicentennial of the Civil War by threatening to kick off its sequel.

He may not quality as Snow White, but Rick is perfectly qualified to replace his odious namesake from Pennsylvania and join the thoroughly unelectable Seven Dwarves, presently competing to carry the Republican banner in 2012. (For a moment there, I thought Ambassador Huntsman had a chance, until he embraced Paul Ryan's "Path To Oblivion")

The question is, how long can the GOP wait for their Prince or Princess Charming to come along and revive their presidential pretensions; or are their chances of ever reconstituting themselves as a viable, national party nothing but a fairy tale?

ARE YOU A DODO?
Bergman's Blog, June 9, 2011

It's time for some perspective on what's going on. What's not going on is Weinergate. Who cares if some horny legislator is Twitting his bulge in cyberspace? What's not going on is whether Evita Palin is going to throw her wink in the ring. What substantive contribution could this ignorant opportunist add to the national debate? What's not going on is the cat and mouse game being played over raising the national debt. What can the Republicans hope to gain, except a further trashing of their already diminished brand by delaying the inevitable?
What is going on is a simultaneous crises in our economy, our environment and our health care and education systems. Wise minds have warned of this gathering storm for decades, but the American public would rather go Dancing With The Stars than Dealing With The Facts.

Just what are the facts? We'll start with the economy. When Obama took office, he inherited an economy that had been trashed by the previous two administrations. Bill Clinton couldn't keep his deregulating pen in his pants. He burned down the firewall between banks and stock jobbers, turning our financial markets into one great, unsupervised casino. Bush The Younger, with the able assistance of Ayn Rand's disciple at the head of the Fed turned Reagan's trickle-down into a floodAnd; and, what treasure Dubya couldn't give away to the rich, he squandered on an illegal war in Babylon.

The child of these depredations is our present, official unemployment rate of 9%, read double that number if you include those too discouraged to look for a job and the legion of skilled professionals taking huge pay and benefit cuts just to snatch a near entry level job. Worse yet is the record number of the unemployed who have been out of work for more than a year. The longer they are denied a job, the less chance they have of ever returning to the workforce. And no one has come to their rescue, save Obama who squeezed a sixteen week extension of unemployment benefits out of the compassion-free GOP in exchange for extending the Bush tax cuts for the wealthy, a plutocratic piñata if ever there was one.

So much for the economy, let's weather the blizzards, wade through the floods and step over the middens of dead birds to talk about the environment. We'll begin with carbon based global warming. Forget the vast body of legitimate research that supports global warming; confronting it would be bad for smokestack industry, would imprison us in four cylinder, girly cars, and, in general, would take exception with American exceptionalism. Furthermore, there's no mention of global warming in any of the myriad editions of the Bible, so it can't be true. While we're turning a scientific calamity into a partisan brouhaha, we're running out of water, poisoning the land with petrochemicals, drilling an ever-widening hole in the ozone layer and killing species right and left, all in the name of living large.

Our health care system is a cruel joke. It's the most costly and least efficient among all the developed nations. Millions are uninsured, living with diseases and chronic conditions, for which only the fortunate are treated. Billions of work hours are lost to unnecessary illness, families are bankrupted by outrageous medical bills, preventive care goes grossly underfunded, America infant mortality ranks 180th out of 224 countries just behind Guam and Cuba and, yet, the health care establishment has propagandized our citizens into loudly defending their right to be sick.

Our education system, like it's health care counterpart is a victim of the same Calvinist analysis-if you weren't born into prosperity, then God has turned his face from you, dooming you to thirteen years (if you last) of scratching out an education in overcrowded, understaffed, ill equipped and often downright dangerous schools.But, you don't need to know if the world is round, if you're watching it all day on a flat screen? Employers are constantly complaining that they can't find qualified personnel to fill key, high text jobs. No surprise. A physicist friend of mind who sits on the Ph.D committee of a major university told me that not one candidate who has come before him in the last twenty years was born in this country.

That's what's going on; so screw the tales of virtual, congressional sex, disregard the posturing of the garden gnomes playing capture the Republican flag and discount the deficit dumb show. We either deepen our analysis, seriously question the shibboleths of conventional wisdom and rise up against the machine or live as dodos and suffer their fate.

PLAN 'B' FOR THE GOP
Bergman's Blog, June 13, 2011

Tim Pawlenty fooled me big time. I had him clocked as the "Sage Of Beige," a typical Midwestern matzoh ponem-Yiddish for a face with all the sizzle of a sheet of matzoh. I was certain that he was more vanilla than killa; but that was before he decided to kiss up bid time to the Tea Party. Remember, Timmy was a tree hugging, tax raising Governor of Minnesota, a giant no-no among the wingnut fringe that has corrupted the heart and soul of the former party of Lincoln, TR and Ike.

So what does T-Paw do to make his right wing bones? He comes up with a plan that makes Paul Ryan look positively Keynesian. Candidate Pawlenty proposes to reduce the top individual tax rate from 35% to 25%, cut the top corporate tax from 25% to 15%, and do away entirely with estate taxes and taxes on capital gains, dividends and interest. According to the Tax Policy Center, Tim's Path To Plutocracy will cost the Treasury 11 billion dollars over the next ten years.

And he's being taken seriously! The GOP is so hooked on the Koch bros, that all the natterings of Nobel economists, Wall Street wizards and other grounded-in-reality professionals go in one ear and out the other. No surprise, since there's precious little inside to stop them.

With T-Paw going postal, Mitt Romney is all that remains of political practicality among the other garden gnomes going for the gold. Herman Cain can deliver pizza and little more, Michelle Bachmann is a shrill, unfunny joke, Ron Paul is a child only Ayn Rand could love, Rick Santorum is a non-starter in his own state and Newt Gingrich is staring down the muzzle of his own loose canon.

Considering the precarious state of their present lineup, I offer the GOP a workable Plan B-don't run anyone in 2012. Concede the election to Obama, and spend your time and money on retaining your majority in the House and taking the Senate. Without the burden of a no-coattails candidate, it just might work.

GUARANTEED SUBSTANCE-FREE

Bergman's Blog, June 16, 2011

The Republican debate last night in New Hampshire is proof positive that the Seven Dwarfs, pledged to making Obama a one term president have not the slightest idea of what to do with an economy sunk in an ongoing depression, and an electorate sunk in a barely conscious malaise.

With the the structurally unemployed growing older as I speak, with a quarter of twenty-somethings looking for jobs that aren't there and with the GNP totally stalled; well, you'd think Romney or any of the lesser lights on stage would have some sort of plan for putting things right. But to them, the unemployed, the uninsured and the uneducated pose no problem as long as they don't indulge in same sex marriage, exercise a woman's right of choice or practice the Muslim faith.

This was just the first of a long line of substance-free debates, chorusing the praises of emasculating Medicare, making the super-rich super richer and calling up the troops for another culture war. I don't think any of these fools have a chance of beating Obama; but one of them, or some other yet undeclared right wing tyro, will get the chance; and, who knows, a bullet, an embolism or a Weinergate squared scandal could put them at the helm. What a nightmare!

It's bad enough that Obama might face another "just say no" Republican House in his second term. That would be sufficient to slow down any recovery to a crawl; but a Romney/Bachmann team or something even more antediluvian in the White House will doom us entirely.

I won't move to Canada because it's too cold, and I can't move to New Zealand because I don't have the six figure entrance fee; so, I'll just stick around and tough it out with the rest of us sub-millionaires, ready to sign up at the drop of a tri-corner cap for the second American Revolution that might just set us free.

WHEN IN DOUBT - STRIDULATE

Bergman's Blog, Previously Unpublished

What does a do-nothing Congress, the Democrats' revenue plan, the demography of America in 2050 and an insect with a singing penis have in common? This cartoon...

THE WEINER WITHDRAWS
Bergman's Blog, Previously Unpublished

One day, it was just on a whim,

He took shots of himself at the gym.

    Then he Tweeted the pics

    To his Las Vegas tricks,

Thank goodness, we got rid of him.

LOST IN THE LOST GENERATION
Bergman's Blog, June 21, 2011

Making nice with the Taliban

Watching the Euro take a Greasy slip and fall

Leaving China in search of the new land of ultra cheap labor

Whamo comes home to the land that hates unions

Paul Krugman and his dismal graph

The Republicans as the new wooly headed Marxists

When will we all paste some on?

FROM FOUNDING TO FOUNDERING FATHERS

Bergman's Blog, June 28, 2011

I am ashamed of the Republicans in Congress for the juvenile, ill-conceived and radically partisan way they are handling what has blossomed into the debt ceiling crisis. I am appalled at the consequences that will ensue if they force the government to publicly consider defaulting on our obligations, let alone actually doing the deed.

How dare they put our financial system and the world economy at risk to promote their misguided and pernicious crusade to shred our safety net, disregard our crumbling infrastructure, sicken our populace and dumb down our children.

I have never been a great fan of Mitch McConnell, and had little reason to familiarize myself with John Boehner; but did presume that both were reasonably informed, well intentioned and fundamentally committed to our nation's economic heath and growth. They have shown themselves to be none of these.

In the thrall of the nattering nativists, mere tea-puppets themselves of the infinitely greedy and thoroughly anti-democratic right; and dependent on these very same odious plutocrats for the loot to run their campaigns, the likes of McConnell and Boehner have sacrificed the spirit of comity and compromise to the idols of cant and calumny.

The founding fathers faced a similar debt crises. Replying to members of the Continental Congress who toyed with default, James Madison reminded them that "Justice, gratitude, our reputation abroad, and our tranquility at home" required provisions be made to honor the debt.

Two centuries later we face the same challenge with less able hands manning the ship of state. The GOP majority in the House and substantial minority in the Senate are, with very few exceptions, a feckless crew of ideologues, theocrats, lackeys and power mongers, who have neither the sand nor the sense to come to terms with the enormity of the debacle they are stage managing.

That their reckless, self-serving handling of the situation may energize a dazed and confused electorate to cast them all to the back benches and oblivion is small consolation for the dishonored and shattered nation they will leave in their wake.

A to Z

An Abecedary For Our Times

By Peter Bergman

Illustrated by Hal O'Dali

A IS AFGHANISTAN, SLIPPING AWAY.
AIN'T NECESSARILY
SOAP
B IS THE BILLIONS WE'LL WASTE IF WE STAY.
C IS THE CONGRESS THAT'S LOCKED IN A STALL
BETTY JO
555-1776
—NEWT
D IS THE DOUBLE DIP FACING US ALL
RECESSION

E IS FOR EGYPT
AND THE MUSCLE THEY FLEXED.

F IS THE FEAR THAT
THE SAUDIS ARE NEXT!

G IS FOR GINGRICH
WHO CHEATS ON HIS WIVES.

H IS THE HORRIBLE THOUGHT
HE
SURVIVES!

NEWT/BACHMANN
2012

KANSAS
KOCHBROS

I IS THE IODINE PILLS THEY MUST TAKE

IN **J** FOR JAPAN WHERE THE NUKES MET THE QUAKE

K IS KADAFI, WHOSE REIGN IS A CRIME

L IS THE LAMPPOST HE'LL SWING FROM IN TIME

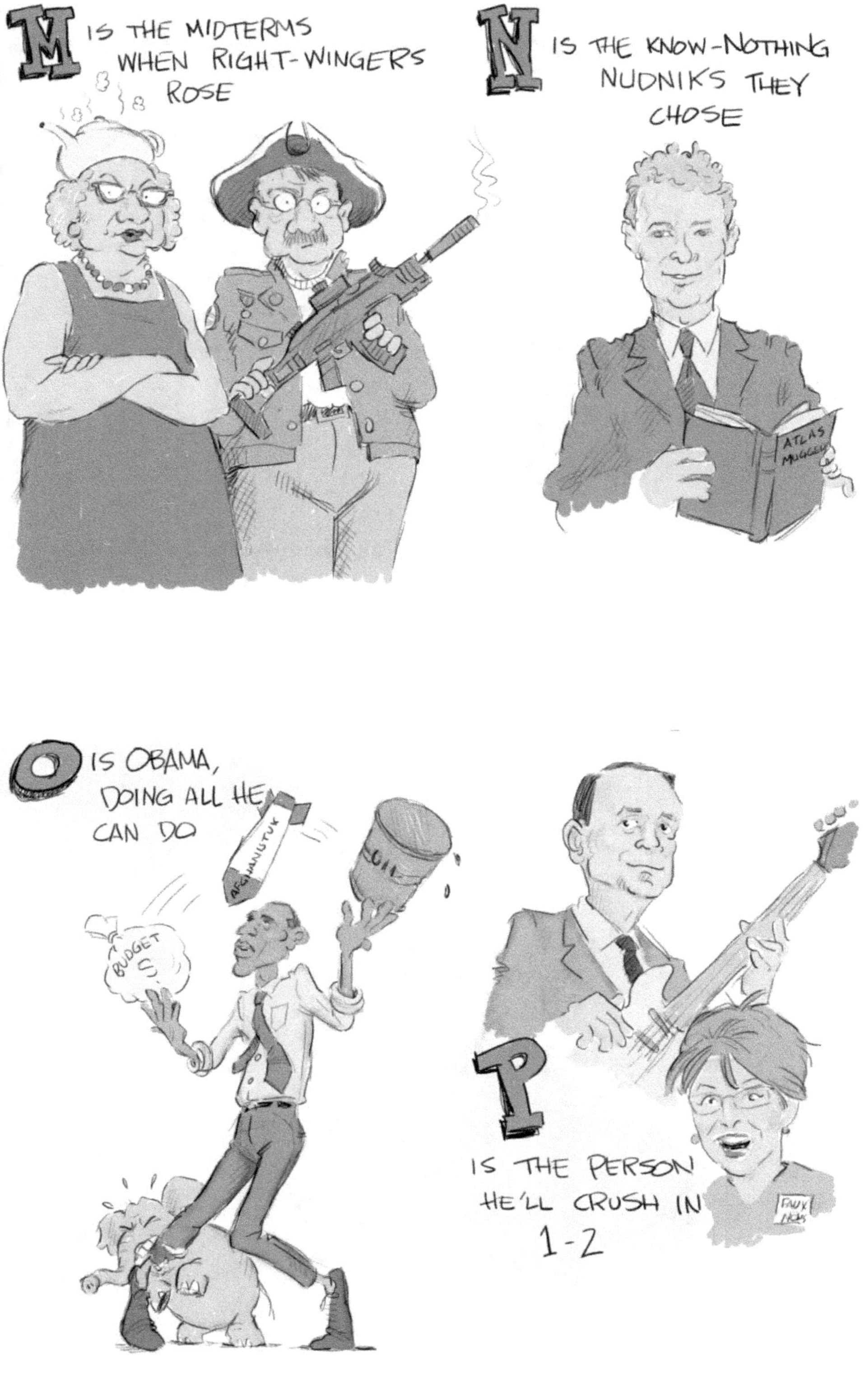

M IS THE MIDTERMS WHEN RIGHT-WINGERS ROSE

N IS THE KNOW-NOTHING NUDNIK'S THEY CHOSE

O IS OBAMA, DOING ALL HE CAN DO

P IS THE PERSON HE'LL CRUSH IN 1-2

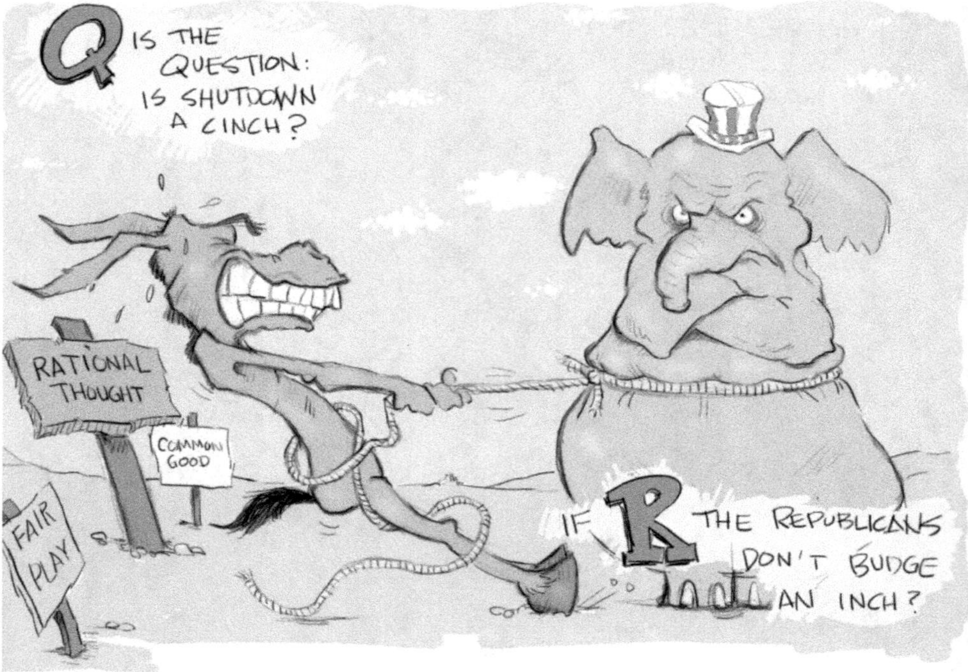
Q IS THE QUESTION: IS SHUTDOWN A CINCH?
RATIONAL THOUGHT
COMMON GOOD
FAIR PLAY
IF R THE REPUBLICANS DON'T BUDGE AN INCH?

S IS THE SUPER-RICH KOCH BROTHER BOYS
DUPE
SLUDGE
T IS THE TEA-PARTY, ONE OF THEIR TOYS

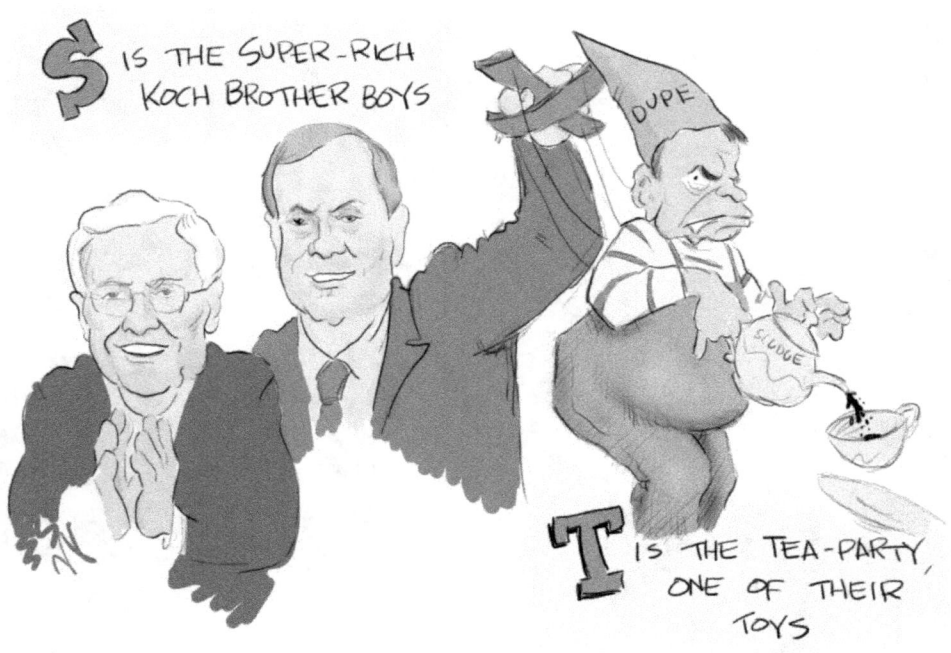

U IS THE UNIONS THAT SCOTT WALKER SCREWED

RECALL

BALLOT BOX

V IS THE VENGEANCE THEY'LL EXACT ON THAT DUDE

W'S THE WALL STREET WE BAILED OUT OF DEBT

X IS THE EXCESSIVE PERKS THEY STILL GET

AND **Y** MUST WE PICTURE
THE INSTINCT TO THRIVE

THE
RONE
RIDERS

MILITARY

KORAN

RELIGION

WALL
STREET

... AS A **Z** ERO SUM GAME
WHERE THE
RUTHLESS
SURVIVE?

THERE'S A MUCH KINDER METHOD FOR REACHING THAT GOAL,
WHERE THE SUM OF THE PARTS QUITE SURPASSES THE WHOLE.

IF WE VISION A FUTURE WHERE EACH HAS A RIGHT
TO A DOCTOR, A TEACHER, AND A WARM BED AT NIGHT.

WE CAN RISE ABOVE FACTION, RACE, GENDER AND CLASS,
AND ENSURE THAT AMERICA'S DREAM COMES TO PASS.

the end

PETER BERGMAN
1939-2012

CODA

As this, the first edition of *Radio Free Oz's Trolling The Woe* was being finalized for print, the Wizard of RFOz, Peter Bergman, passed away in Los Angeles from a rare form of leukemia at age 72.

What you hold in your hands (or are currently viewing on the *device du jour*) is one of Mr. Bergman's last projects seen to fruition under his supervision.

I know it was his wish that this humble little tome chronicling a few months of our country's political histrionics reach the readers it was intended for – And, here you are.

What follows is the transcript of the last words he spoke on his Radio Free Oz podcast just two days before venturing off to parts not quite known.

-30-

-Phil (Hal O'Dali) Fountain
San Francisco, April, 2012

Take heart, dear friends.
We are passing through the darkening of the light.
We're gonna make it and we're going to make it together.
Don't get ground down by cynicism.
Don't let depression darken the glass through which you look.
This is a garden we live in.
A garden seeded with unconditional love.
And the tears of the oppressed,
and the tears of the frustrated,
and the tears of the good will spring those seeds.
The flag has been waved.
It says occupy.
Occupy Wall Street.
Occupy the banks.
Occupy the nursing homes.
Occupy Congress.
Occupy the big law offices.
Occupy the lobbyists.
Occupy…yourself.
Because that's were it all comes together.
I pledge to you, from this moment on, whatever it means, I'm going to occupy myself.
I love ya.
See you tomorrow.

-Peter Bergman
March, 2012

www.ingramcontent.com/pod-product-compliance
Lightning Source LLC
Chambersburg PA
CBHW051144020726
47501CB00005B/1675